KAI'S *Healing* SMILES

VIVI ANNE HUNT

Edited by B. K. Bass.
Layout by Atticus.
Book cover by Vivi Anne Hunt.
Original art by Ruart.

First paperback edition 2022.
Paperback: 978-619-92273-0-5
Ebook: 978-619-92273-1-2

Published by Vivi Anne Hunt
Ruse 7012, Bulgaria
viviannehunt.com

To my parents, who always supported this dream.

To my best friend, who always got my back.

And to the real-life angels out there who come to us in mysterious ways and heal us with their smiles.

Thank you.

Contents

$\mathscr{Blurb}$

Can a smile heal a broken heart?

Silas is mourning the loss of his wife. Every day, he is going through the motions and barely managing to keep the excruciating pain from overtaking his life. There is precisely one ray of sunshine in his days — Kai — the smiley, awkward barista at Starbucks. For some reason, Silas finds comfort in being around Kai and soaks up as much light as this sweet boy could give him.

For the short time Kai has worked at Starbucks, he has secretly watched one man from afar, hoping that one day he would notice him back. He looks all mature, business-like, and always sad. One day Kai finally gets the chance to speak to him. And this is where their story begins.

Will Silas be able to let go of the past and start fresh? And will Kai be able to heal the gloomy man with his smiles?

Comission
Ruart

Chapter 1

SILAS

Losing a soulmate is like losing two limbs, or all of them at once. Suddenly, you don't know what to do with your body. You go through life like a zombie, with infrequent flashes of awareness which anchor you to the world around you, if you're lucky.

For me, that flash was Kai.

However, before we can talk about Kai, we have to talk about coffee.

Even though I could afford it, Starbucks always seemed overpriced. Ellie and I argued about it endlessly. She would drag me inside and make me order the most ridiculous drinks with the most ridiculous names and pay a ridiculous price for the privilege of imbibing at that shrine to the holy bean.

After she was gone, Starbucks was the only place I went for my coffee. I would torture myself, recounting every conversation we had ever had inside, then go home with tear stains on my cheeks and a hole in my heart.

Despite that, I would go back. One day as I walked inside, before I even smelled the brewing coffee, I saw him. A new barista. Kai. Out of nowhere, this young, outgoing, smiling creature with a bright smile and eyes appeared—and he never left. For five months, he has been the only shot of energy I've needed. He is my color and light throughout my gray days.

I start my day with Kai and finish it with... well, staring at a photo of me and Ellie. The only one I kept in our bedroom.

Ellie was also one of those people who always smiled, like she had a string that constantly pulled at the corners of her lips, for it was painful for her to stay serious or angry. She would switch after moments of untypical emotion and that was it.

I missed that, so I was thankful for Kai.

"Morning, Silas," he beamed each morning; as if I were a good reason to smile, but I knew better. He said everyone's name and had a smile for them, so I wasn't special.

I still liked it.

So, I went to Starbucks every day and ordered all their ridiculous drinks, a different one each day. Some people gave me strange looks, but I didn't care. I told myself I was doing it for Ellie. In truth, I kept going to see Kai's bright smile. Then, coffee in hand and a little light in my heart, I would go to work designing blueprints for an architectural firm. What else is there to do after you lose your soulmate? You just bury yourself in whatever you can find to keep you busy and you don't stick out your head for anything.

It was one of those days, a Friday, and I was meeting my best friend, Wesley, for coffee. I was surprised he was still my best friend since I only half-listened to him. I suppose he was giving me the benefit of the doubt because he knew how much losing Ellie destroyed me. Maybe he had more hope for me than I did.

"Iced white chocolate mocha, please," I said automatically, following the roster.

The cashier smiled and took my money, then Kai smiled, as always, and started making my drink with such deft movements that I couldn't help but stare. Next to me, Wesley, otherwise known as Wes, frowned.

We didn't usually meet there, but he asked about my Starbucks habit for some reason, so there we were. Once our drinks were ready, we sat at a table, me with my ridiculously overpriced and named beverage and him frowning at me.

"What?" I asked.

"Nothing," he said, shrugging. "I just thought..."

"What? Spit it out."

"You know what." He smiled. "Never mind. How's work going?"

That's all he asked about these days because he knew I had no personal life.

"Good. Fine. My clients seem happy."

He snorted into his mocha latte. Wes always drank the same thing. He was taller than me, with muscles for days and tattoos peeking out of every crevice of his clothing. The lucky bastard was a tattoo artist with his own tattoo parlor.

We met in college, where I also met Ellie. When she died, he was as devastated as I was, but he moved on because he still had all of his limbs, while mine still felt numb.

"How's that new one, Nathaniel, treating you?" he asked with a smirk, because he knew Nathaniel Mars was the bane of my existence. He had asked me to revise the blueprints twice already, and I was sensing a third time coming.

I groaned. "Why ask when you know the answer?"

"Because I like to see you squirm, of course."

I sensed a foreign presence at my back, so I turned my head to see Kai wiping the tables. He was pretending to ignore us, but I noticed him looking at Wes from time to time. Something strange sparked in my stomach, but it went out almost immediately.

A blip.

Wes cocked his head, frowning at me.

I sighed. "What? You're acting like a nut today."

"Nuts, eh? Is that what they put in coffees these days?"

I ignored his smirk and sipped my coffee, feeling nothing. To be honest, it was one of the worse tasting ones on the menu, but again: I didn't do it for me—I did it for Ellie.

Wes frowned at my drink like it had accosted him. "Do you still order everything on the menu?"

I shrugged.

"When are you going to stop torturing yourself?"

I shook my head, unwilling to get into it, even with my best friend. He was the kind of person who didn't mince his words, but sometimes I just needed someone who understood, damn it.

He sighed, then looked behind me and smiled. "You like tats?"

Behind me, in the corner of my eye, Kai jumped like a startled, skittish animal. I turned around to take all of him in as he tried to regain his composure.

"Oh, shoot... sorry," he said, still smiling. "Didn't mean to stare. It's just that you have some good ones on you."

"Thanks," Wes said. "Do you have any?"

I wondered why Wes was being nice to a virtual stranger, but then again, he was more social than I ever was.

"No. Not yet, anyway," Kai said. "Where did you get yours?"

"JustInk. Have you ever been?"

"No, but I hear it's great. My mate was there last month."

"Cool," Wes said with a relaxed smile. "You should come check it out. I work there."

"Wow, awesome," Kai said. "I didn't know Silas had such cool friends." He seemed to catch what he said and his eyes widened. "I mean, of course you'd have cool friends," he said to me. "Fuck—I mean fudge... What am I saying? I'll shut up now. Sorry." He walked away, flushing up to his ears.

Something about his embarrassment brought a huge grin and a chuckle out of me.

Wesley looked at me like I had grown an alien appendage all of a sudden.

"Fucking hell," I grunted. "What now?"

"You're smiling."

"So?"

"So, I haven't seen you smile since... you know."

I shook my head, refusing to talk about it. "I smile sometimes. It's not a big deal and definitely not something you should alert the media about."

He narrowed his eyes and stared as he mulled that over. "Okay, then." He relaxed. "Now, tell me all about this Nathaniel fellow, and leave no stone unturned."

I rolled my eyes. It was fun for him to torture me, so I told him everything.

From that day on, we met at Starbucks every morning.

***

KAI

Was it a friend or a boyfriend, though? I'd seen them together a few times since that first encounter, and I still couldn't tell.

Like many other days, I hid behind the muffin stand and spied on Silas and his tatted-up god of a man, wondering what the fuck I was doing with my life. Pathetically, I spied and, when I could, eavesdropped on customers.

Well, one customer in particular.

"Are you still mooning over your man?" May asked, cackling like a bloody witch. "What's it been, a year?"

"Shut up," I muttered. "I'm doing no such thing."

"Uh-huh, and I'm a dummy who can't tell the difference."

"Did you come here to gloat because you have a gorgeous girlfriend who talks to you and touches you with no intermediaries, like coffee cups? And it's been half a year, not that anyone is counting."

"Of course not," she said, laughing. "Why don't you go talk to him? I mean, what's the worst that can happen?"

"Uh, he could be straight, or that could be his boyfriend."

She sighed. "So? Then you know, and you're free to moon over other customers."

"You're hilarious. And annoying. Maybe you should go do your job now."

"Maybe you should do yours," she said, sticking out her pierced tongue. May was one of those girls who didn't give a damn what the manager said, so she refused to remove it or to dye her purple hair back to blond. Since the boss liked it, our manager, Stew, had to tolerate her.

That was a relief for me because her sarcasm sustained me on most days.

"I mean, if I were a gay guy," she said, deep in thought as she played with her piercing, "I would go for that tatted-up titan. No offense."

"None taken," I said, looking at the back of Silas' neck. It was nice and strong, matching his nice, strong body. Not to mention his strong hands, his forearms... Jesus, I was losing the plot. I really was pathetic.

Silas was one of those men who always looked meticulous, not a hair out of place. And he dressed like he had money, so I had no idea why a man like that would gaze at scrawny little me. Thinking he was there for anything but the coffee was officially sad.

Nothing was going to happen.

Unfortunately, he was just my type—older than me, brooding, with a nice smile when he shared it and a solid body. A body that could protect me and do dirty things to me and—

"Hey, it's Kai, right?"

Holy shit, I'd been fantasizing about a customer and now I was caught red-handed. I stared at Silas' friend or boyfriend, waiting to be told off. He surely didn't like me looking at his man, drooling all over myself.

"Uh, yeah," I stammered, probably going red. Damn skin, always revealing everything I'm thinking.

"Haven't seen you at JustInk yet. Or did you decide to go another way?" he asked, smirking like he knew something.

"Oh, shit—I mean shoot. I haven't had the time, I guess, but I was planning to stop by this month. You work there, right?"

"I run the place."

"Whoa, you run the place? Jesus, no wonder—" *Oh my god, shut up.*

"No wonder what?"

"Nothing," I muttered. "And yeah, I'll stop by. I like your style." *Even though you have stolen the one guy I'd been interested in since forever.* Well, there were other guys. There were always other guys, but they were mostly commitment-phobes, straight-passing guys who wanted me to hide in their closets, or guys like me who liked the same kind of unobtainable fruit and were so hard up for sex they settled for me.

Twenty-five was too old for this shit.

"Cool, you do that," he said, still smirking. Why was he smirking?

I let others serve him because his weird attention freaked me out. Why did he want me to go to his shop, and why was he looking at me like that? Did he know something? Was he smug because I drooled over his boyfriend?

Jesus, Kai, you're losing the plot again.

"Aww, too bad it was the other one, otherwise I would have said, 'well done,'" May said, barely containing her manic laughter.

"Gee, thanks," I muttered. "Some progress, huh?"

"You know, maybe you should look at it this way: If his boyfriend likes you, you can do a menage type thing together." She waggled her eyebrows.

"God, go away and leave me alone. Don't you have some incense to burn or something?" Did I mention? May was a witch. A real fucking witch in this day and age, and I was fascinated by that. Also terrified because I didn't want to be the subject of her creepy spells or voodoo dolls.

Granted, I had no idea how it worked, but I'd seen movies like The Craft or that TV show, Charmed. They told me all I needed to know.

"Okay, here's the new plan. You go to this guy's tattoo place—"

"Eavesdrop much?"

"And you ask discretely about your man. What's the worst that can happen?"

"He can punch me for having the hots for his boyfriend?"

"Or he can kiss you, fall into bed with you, and you two begin a beautiful life together. Seriously, dump the other one and hook up with this one. Even a freaking lesbian can see that he's packing."

I rolled my eyes. May was such a meddler. "I don't like... all that."

"What exactly do you like?"

Yeah, like I was going to tell her. "Don't you have an eye of newt to cook up? Or, wait, let me guess: You secretly add your witchy stuff to people's orders."

Now she cackled. "Aww, man. That would be fun. I could solve the world's problems, one overpriced cup at a time."

"You mean you'd cure cancer and reverse climate change?"

"Nah, I'll just turn assholes into sweethearts and sweethearts into assholes. You know, shake things up. It would give everyone perspective."

"Sounds like a wonderful disaster waiting to happen, and a lovely Hollywood blockbuster."

"See, you get me." She leaned in to whisper as if sharing a conspiracy. "And if you ever need a love spell, I'm your girl."

I groaned. "I need a love spell like I need fungus on my foot."

We kept bantering as we worked. It was a slow Saturday afternoon, so there wasn't much else to do. Later, when Silas and his friend or boyfriend were leaving, the tatted-up monster of a man winked at me, at which point I probably blushed like an idiot. *Again*.

"See, babe? You got it in the bag." May elbowed me.

I sighed and cursed my luck. They were probably a couple looking for some twinks to play with or something. I hated having to share, or being one of many, but somehow the guys I liked always wanted that.

Oh, well. Back to reality.

Chapter 2

SILAS

After more than a decade working at Future & Past Designs, I was one of three chief architects who had their picks of the best projects. The well-paid ones. Too bad those sometimes came with strings such as nightmare clients.

Ellie would have waved her delicate hand and said something that would turn my perspective around. She would smile and say something like, *Life comes with gifts, but they are never free.* I think she said that once. Also, she would be proud of me for rising to the top when so many others tried to do that every year and failed.

However, I only did it because I had nothing else to do but work.

Those other people must have had lives.

"Sir?" my assistant asked through the com. "Nathaniel Mars is here to see you."

Of course he would come unannounced.

"Let him in."

Nathaniel Mars was a tall, lean man with expensive taste in clothing. His shirts probably cost more than my suits. He had a neatly trimmed beard and eyes full of humor that was always at your expense.

Whatever.

I worked with the guy; I didn't have to marry him.

"Mr. Mars," I said. "To what do I owe this distinct pleasure?"

He rolled his eyes. He was onto me. "I saw the latest revisions, and I must say, there's an improvement." He sat down on the chair facing me and steepled his fingers on my desk.

"But?" I guessed.

"But I would like more work on the garden."

"Meaning?"

"Meaning I don't want it to look like a maze from one of those young adult bestsellers of late. I want something more..."

Traditional. Boring. The same as everyone else's.

"...tasteful."

Ah, of course, another synonym for boring. "I'll see what I can do."

He gave me a sweeping look, frowning. "Do you ever smile, Silas?" This was the first time he'd used my first name, which was jarring.

"I do, when the situation warrants it."

He squinted. "I see. Well, you have my number." There was quite a bit of ice in his tone, then he left me watching after his Armani-clad ass.

This is the time when I should probably admit that I am bisexual. Before Ellie, I enjoyed both men and women equally with great pleasure.

After her... Well, after her, I didn't enjoy anything at all. It was like being castrated on top of losing all my limbs. I felt like a brain on a stick on most days, unable to enjoy anything on a physical level. The anti-depressants didn't help the issue.

Perhaps I shouldn't have taken out my frustration on Nathaniel, but he'd made me do more revisions than any of our past clients. At some point, I would have to put my foot down or even send him away, losing money. Not that the partners would let me. No, maybe someone else would take him on. At that thought, I felt a lightness in my chest.

Could I possibly toss him to someone else? Jesus, what was I thinking? It would be a huge payout, which meant I'd finally be able to get that house Ellie had liked so much. I promised her we would get it, so now I wanted to get it for her.

Thus, I would have to give the man his boring garden.

After work, I headed off to my favorite Starbucks and ordered the next drink on the menu. I had started going twice a day a couple of months back for some reason. I didn't have to go twice, but Kai was always there with his perennial smile and big eyes; I had to admit, having something to look forward to made me want to go twice, so I did.

After all, my home was empty and my life was empty, so I might as well grasp at any straws that life was kind enough to provide me.

Kai was slumped behind some muffins, doodling something in a sketchbook. I hadn't seen it before, so I stretched my neck and squinted. I usually wore glasses to see fine details, but right then, my eyes were naked.

"Wow, that's stunning," I said without thinking.

It was a gorgeous drawing of a man with a vine tattoo wrapping around his entire body like barbed wire. It was ingenious, really.

Kai's head shot up and his eyes went wide. As always, his face went red right up to his ears when he got embarrassed. I didn't mean to embarrass him; I just really liked the drawing. He appeared to be a very talented young man.

"Fuck," he cursed. "I mean fudge. I, uh, I wasn't slacking off or anything." He closed his sketchbook, hiding it from sight.

"It's a hobby, nothing more. Just doodles. Doodling helps me relax. At work. Where I should be working." He closed his eyes and his flush deepened. "Shit—I mean shoot."

I burst out laughing, maybe for the first time since I lost Ellie. Still wide-eyed, Kai smiled nervously. "Sorry."

"Don't apologize. You're very talented. Do you do tattoos as well?"

He shook his head. "God, no. I've never done that. It costs a fortune to learn, and anyway, I would probably maim someone for life, or I could bleed them to death accidentally, like they did in the old days, with leeches, thinking it was healing and not, well, unsanitary." He sighed. "Sorry, I babble when I'm nervous."

"Why are you nervous, Kai?"

He froze.

"What? Is there something wrong?"

"You know my name. Wow, cool. That was... weird. I mean, I'm the one who's weird right now. Fudge, sorry, did you want a drink or something?"

I laughed at his discomfort, not that I was some sadist or some such, but it was cute how he babbled on mindlessly. The more time I spent with him, the more I realized he was one of those unspoiled individuals, the ones the world should protect, the ones who not only helped, but saved those of us who were lost.

He helped me with his smiles.

God, I'd been a jerk. Being around Kai helped me, and I was just mooching off him like a vampire while giving nothing in return. *Maybe...* "My friend Wesley has a tattoo parlor, you know. JustInk? I'm sure he would agree to mentor you or have one of his guys do it."

"Friend? Huh?" He blinked a few times. "Oh, no, I couldn't—what?"

I felt myself smiling. I was definitely smiling, which I wasn't exactly known for, but how else does one respond to such unblemished radiance?

"Would you like me to ask Wes if he'd be willing to do that?"

Kai shook his head, looking dazed. "I... wow... I mean, if it's not too much trouble, you know? You don't have to do that."

"I want to. You are talented, and I have a friend who can help."

"Okay," he said, gifting me with his brilliant smile, albeit it was a bit shy. "Thanks, Silas."

"Sure, kid. Now, can I get a blonde vanilla latte, please?"

His smile dimmed. "Yes, right away."

***

KAI

Yeah, it wasn't happening in this lifetime.

He looked straight at me and called me *kid*, like one would call a pet or something. Jesus. Was I really that young-looking? Or was he so much older than I thought? He couldn't have been older than thirty-something, right? Or a good-looking forty-something.

My delirious happiness at him noticing me and talking to me, then even offering to help me, was quickly replaced by disappointment.

I had to stop mooning over him.

Probably.

"Here you go," I said, handing him his drink with a smile.

He smiled back, which took me off guard because he didn't smile often. "Thanks, Kai, for everything."

I frowned. What did *that* mean?

Before he left, he turned around. "I'll let you know what Wes says, all right?"

"Okay, thanks," I said, for lack of anything else to say. When he was finally gone, I slumped against the counter. I had the worst luck with men and the worst taste. If you threw me in a literal sea of men, I would find the ones who were the worst choices, every time.

Fudge.

The afternoon picked up after that with the wave of people heading home from work and I buried myself in orders, trying not to think about the day's events. When my shift ended, I headed out the back to my bike. It was locked on the bike rack, looking alone and sad. Most people drove there, but I couldn't afford a car.

The ride home took about twenty minutes, as always. I was careful on the way, avoiding busy roads. My mother's voice always warned me to be careful of cars while cycling. She even played me clips of horrid accidents with cars that ran over cyclists.

It worked.

I lived with two other guys: Jason, who was always high, and Parker, who was either always out or home with a girl. It was awkward to have to do anything under the soundtrack of moans and chicks screaming and sounding like they were shooting a porno movie, but I got used to it.

Girls are so much louder in bed.

Anyway, Jason and I got on well enough. I wasn't into drugs, so I always said no when he offered. He mostly smoked pot and had this dazed look about him, but he was also funny and relaxed, which worked for me.

Like always, I found him doing yoga.

"Ah, you found it... the missing link in the human body," I joked when I saw him bent in on himself like a pretzel, making me wonder if he could suck his own dick. I'd heard there were people who could do that.

Jason chuckled and unpretzeled himself. Anybody else might be annoyed that I interrupted them, but he always went with the flow. "That last one, man, I was out of this world, you know?"

"Uh huh," I said, having no experience with being on any other worlds. "Did anything come for me?"

He shrugged.

I went to the mail table and checked, but there were just bills and Parker's stupid catalogues, which he never took, so they kept piling up.

Sighing, I went to sit on the sofa.

"Why the long face?" Jason asked. "Is your boyfriend sending you stuff again?"

I rolled my eyes. "He's not my boyfriend, Geez, I've told you this a hundred times. We just chat a lot on the forums, and he just happened to have that graphic novel I wanted but couldn't find in a store."

Jason nodded, looking serene as usual. "Boyfriends send each other special gifts like that. Are you sure he's just a friend?"

"Of course he is. He lives in England. You know, across the pond, so we can never even meet in person. Liking him that way would be dumb, and on most days, I try not to be so dumb."

"Okay, okay, I hear ya. So, how's your other boyfriend?"

"You're delightful today, you know that?" I went to get something to drink from the fridge. It was our ritual to have a chat as soon as I came home. "He, uh... I mean, he actually spoke to me today."

"Whoa! Congrats, man. So, when are you seeing him again?"

"He saw me drawing and suggested his friend could mentor me at JustInk."

Jason's eyes went wide, to what most people's eyes looked like. "No shit? Today's your day. Have you tried playing the lotto?"

"Not really. I don't need money. I just need to like someone who actually likes me back for once." I let out a deep sigh, then winced as a memory from the day came streaking back to the forefront of my mind. "He called me a kid."

Jason snorted.

"It's not funny," I muttered. "It was so embarrassing."

"He probably likes you but doesn't know it yet. Like, when I met you, I had my doubts, but now we're as tight as buns."

"Uh, thanks? Why did you have your doubts?"

"You smile too much. You do it when you're nervous, too. It's jarring."

I laughed, taking a sip of my energy drink. "Seriously? Is smiling really that jarring? I thought it was something people liked."

"Crazy people smile too much."

"Okay, Rain Man, I get it. I'll try to tone it down."

I thought about what he said. Did I really smile too much? I didn't realize. At work, you're supposed to smile at the customers, but I was at home. Maybe I did it subconsciously to avoid getting into fights? In high school, I tried my best to hide from the bigger guys who picked on guys my size. My mom once told me to try to smile and see if that worked. It did, if only because it confused the fuckers, so maybe I started doing it full-time.

"Is it like... a creepy smile?"

"You mean like the Joker's? Or like the Cheshire Cat's?"

"Either one."

"Nah, man, it's like that bashful shit people do when they're stealing out of the cookie jar and want to distract you from the fact."

"So, you're saying I smile like a kid?"

"Yeah," Jason said in triumph, making me groan. No wonder Silas thought I was a kid; I was giving him the wrong signals.

Damn it.

Jason continued, "Well, sometimes you smile like Heath Ledger in 10 Things I Hate About You. Like, it doesn't reach your eyes, but it's still cute."

"Wow."

"And sometimes you smile like Mona Lisa, like you have a secret."

I blinked at Jason, who was now lounging on the sofa next to me with a serene face and sprawled legs. "Any reason why you have cataloged my smiles?"

"Hmm, maybe I'm in love with you."

I snort. "Maybe you're full of shit."

"I bet your man likes your smiles. Trust me, there's no way not to like them. That would be like kicking a puppy. It's just sad."

"So, what you're saying is that I have a puppy smile, like a kid's, and that anyone who kicks me is just sad. Thanks for that."

"You're welcome," he said with a wink. "I'm a fountain of wisdom."

"You're a fountain of something," I said, laughing, then headed into my room to catch up with Simon.

Simon and I met on the Geeklandia forums, where geeks discuss their favorite fandoms. Simon's was Game of Thrones, and mine was Doctor Who. You might think those don't go together, but geeks like variety, and these forums celebrate that fact. As a result, Simon had made me watch some Game of Thrones while I made him watch Doctor Who. It was fun.

Killed time.

I didn't do much other than go to work and draw, really, so I'd taken up the forums as a mindless hobby. We don't have a TV at the apartment, and even though I planned to take night classes, I still couldn't manage it, what with the long shifts at Starbucks and the high-sky expenses.

Living in the city was tough.

Tired after a long day of work, I plopped on my bed and opened my laptop, propping my head on one arm while opening the Geeklandia page. The message icon said I had new messages, so I opened my mailbox.

Well, geekbox.

That episode where the Doctor goes back in time to save himself from himself was so meta, I loved it. Why am I not surprised it's your favorite?

But I really thought the next one was rubbish and stopped watching, going back to the familiar naked women and beheadings.

The doctor needs more of those.

I laughed at one of Simon's smaller tangents.

Don't forget the incest slash twincest, I typed, *and the naked men, which is the only reason I even tolerate this crazy show.*

He responded right away. *Yes, flapping tiny dicks is all the rage these days.*

I barked a laugh, still not sure whether Simon was straight or gay or what. We didn't talk about that part of our lives, though he had mentioned a girlfriend once, I think. I typed, *You're getting me hot just thinking about it.*

Obviously, I was not shy about admitting my sexual preferences. I always did it with friends, and if they didn't like it, they could piss off.

Simon typed, *As for the incest, is it weird I find it hot? The whole taboo thing? Basically, GoT takes everything people try not to stare at too hard at and puts it out to the front. Shines a light on it. I bloody love it.*

I rolled my eyes. *That's because you're a freak.*

Thanks, boo, I love you too.

When he said strange things like that, I really wondered what his deal was, but it didn't matter. He was in another country, on another continent. I didn't even know what he looked like, just what show he watched, that he had an avatar with a dragon on it, and that he was a guy.

Or could he be a girl?

I didn't know, and it didn't really matter.

For the rest of the evening, I chatted with Simon, then took a shower and passed out in bed, only to wake up at six am and start all over: clean up, breakfast, coffee, work, and a certain someone I liked to watch secretly.

Someone who apparently saw me as a kid.

Bugger.

Chapter 3

SILAS

The design for Nathaniel's boring garden was done, so I was—finally—conferring with our contractor. I had gone to Nathaniel's Estate, which spanned several miles of woods surrounding his gossamer mansion. It was like a thing from movies, but more modern somehow. Not covered in ivy, anyway.

Nathaniel didn't need an overhaul of his estate, but he wanted one, being the trust fund baby of a rich family. Old money, apparently. He also did a lot of charity, which is how I'd met him a year before at a gala my partners forced me to go to.

After Ellie, I wasn't big on social events since I wouldn't bring anyone else, but when your bosses look at you like they're wondering why they have you there in the first place, you have to swallow your heart, put on a penguin suit, and meet someone who will become your arch nemesis.

That's the story, anyway.

Nathaniel had a maid, a butler, and everything. It was one of his family's estates, so he had it all to himself. I was wishing he could open a brothel or something because he was so uptight. That would have been fun.

"Silas," a deep voice called.

I steeled myself to meet Nathaniel in all his glory—a cashmere suit, a fancy colored shirt, lavender today, and not one hair out of place.

"Mr. Mars," I said.

"Call me Nathaniel, since we'll be working together."

Actually, I would be working with the contractor and the city, and not so much with the client, but I didn't correct him. I added a mental note that if he wanted more changes, he might as well add another million to the deal, which, sadly, he might have agreed to already.

"What can I do for you?"

"Come have tea with me," he said, then walked away as if expecting me to follow. I looked at the contractor, Joe, who was trying not to laugh. He had a family, two kids, a beautiful wife, and a good sense of humor, which is what you need when you work with all kinds of people.

He could withstand the demon because he had patience, as well.

I had... nothing. Nothing to give anyone. I still felt dead on most days, so I just went through life like it was a dream. Some moments were brighter than others, like the moments that brought me joy or annoyed me greatly. Everything else was filler.

"English tea? Black? Green?"

"English, please," I said.

He waved his hand and his maid complied. Jesus, some people. He couldn't even pour himself a cup of tea? Then again, he lived a different life.

"Are you happy with the project so far?" he asked.

I frowned. "I think it's you who needs to be happy, Mr. Mars."

"Nathaniel, please. And I'm asking because sometimes it seems as though... you don't quite enjoy your work. Is that right?"

I enjoyed my work; I didn't enjoy him.

"I enjoy my work just fine." I sipped my tea. Not bad. It was the kind that didn't need any additives because it was rich and lush on its own.

"And your personal life?"

I blinked. "Excuse me?"

"Well, I have never seen you with a wife or a husband," he said, like it was a normal thing to say to someone, "so I decided to ask."

"Mr. Mars—"

"Nathaniel."

"I appreciate your concern for my personal life, but I assure you, I keep it separate from my professional one. Is that all?"

He looked away, sighing. "Yes, that is all, Silas."

I left without finishing my tea, rattled by the man's interest in me. I didn't want to think what it meant because I viewed him as a person I worked with, a professional relationship, and there he would always remain.

On my way back into the city, I called Wes.

"Hey," he said. "What's my favorite friend doing?"

"You mean only friend?" I teased.

He was one of those people everybody liked, so he had many friends, though he insisted they were only acquaintances and real friends had to earn the privilege. Something I happened to agree with.

"You sound cheerful," Wes said. "Did you drop that fancy bastard with the hoity-toity name?"

"No, I'm still stuck with him, unfortunately. Listen, I wanted to talk to you about something. I was going to call yesterday, but I forgot."

"I'm listening." There was a buzzing sound.

"Jesus, are you working and talking?"

"Don't be absurd. I am just lovingly staring into the point of the needle. It is in these moments that I feel the sharp edge as it cuts into the flesh—"

"Please stop. I know it has to be a quote from a movie, but it's disturbing."

He chuckled. "It's not from a movie. It's from my brilliant mind, actually."

"Whatever it's from, I would rather do without it, thanks," I said. "Seriously, I wanted to ask if you had any space for an apprentice at JustInk."

"Why? Have someone in mind?"

"You know that kid, Kai, from Starbucks? Turns out he's quite talented, and he mentioned he'd love to learn, but it's too expensive for him."

Silence.

"Wes, are you there?"

"That guy, the skinny one with the weird smile and the babbling gene? That one?"

"Yeah," I said. "I know you probably don't have the time or space or whatever, but can you at least look at his portfolio and, I don't know, maybe see if anyone from your circles needs an apprentice?"

The buzzing stopped. "Yeah, okay."

"That easy?"

There was rustling and laughter. "God, *yes*, I said. For you, I would do it. For anyone else, they would have to go through Fluffy."

Their accountant's actual name was Maurice, but they called him Fluffy, after the three-headed dog in Harry Potter, because he held the purse strings so tightly no one could even do a pro bono deal without being caught and yelled at.

I laughed. "Man, you'll have trouble with Fluffy."

"Don't I know it," he rumbled. "Hey, you know... uh, I'm happy for you."

"What does that mean?"

"I don't know, just... the fact that you're taking an interest in someone."

I started. "It's not like that. I'm just helping a kid."

"I know, but still. I'm happy."

"Okay..." I was unnerved by how strange Wes sounded. He never minced words or held anything back, but I could feel he wasn't saying something. "Well, thanks. Should I just send him over there after work tomorrow, or...?"

"Yeah, perfect. Send him after seven."

"All right. Thanks, Wes."

"Anytime."

After the bizarre conversation, I thought about what Wes said. He was happy for me because I was taking an interest in something. No, he said *someone*. I had always been like this before, when Ellie was alive. I tried my best to help anyone who was in a lurch or needed a favor, even if it was a small one. Helping people with groceries, finding people jobs or apartments through friends, the whole deal.

It used to drive Ellie mad.

But I hadn't even thought about other people, maybe other than Wes and my family, in a long fucking time.

It didn't matter. Kai was a ray of sunshine who helped me with his daily doses of happiness, and I wanted to return the favor.

That's all it was.

***

KAI

Saturday was always the busiest day. May and I practically had to fly around and managed to fudge up a couple of orders, but covered it quickly. We had each other's backs. Thank the gods for her.

It was so busy I didn't even see Silas was in line, waiting to put in his order. When I noticed him, he looked... different.

I couldn't put my finger on it. He wore the usual fancy pants and fancy shoes and fancy coat with leather gloves, which he held in his hands after taking them off. His hair was combed back and his face was openly looking around at the people, which struck me as odd. I stood there, frozen, like an idiot, watching Silas look around like he'd never done before.

Usually, he walked in, got his coffee, sat down, and drank it.

He seemed to have tunnel vision, but because he looked at me at least, I didn't mind it. That time, he was looking at others, and it seemed out of character. He even gave his spot to a young mother with her little kid.

Wow, that was nice.

Could he be any more perfect?

Fudge, stop that.

I shook my head and focused on a man in front of me who looked murderous and said he'd already ordered, but I was obviously not listening.

My face heating, I focused on his order and went through everyone until Silas reached the counter, smiling. Not a brilliant smile, but a small one. The one I liked to see on his face on the rare occasions he gave it.

He'd given it the first time he showed up, then frowned for the rest of the month for some reason. Then, he showed it from time to time, only when I was around, which made me feel special even though I knew that was ridiculous. Of course, he was smiling because of other things—maybe his thoughts or memories or even the weather. Not me.

I shook my head, dispelling my thoughts. "Hey, Silas, a dark roast coffee today?"

He smiled a little brighter and said, "Yes, thank you."

I'd figured out what he was doing recently, but I always let him order, anyway. I didn't want to assume, even though today I threw that to the wind. He even seemed a bit bashful when I suggested it.

Focus, Kai. He thinks you're a kid. Stop crushing on him.

He paid, leaving a generous tip in the jar, and moved on to the waiting station. After that, I had to work non-stop for about thirty minutes to service everyone. When we finally had a lull, I released a deep breath and looked at May.

She was smirking. "You notice anything?"

I frowned and looked around. Silas was still there. "Oh," I said stupidly.

"I think it's time you took a break."

"Is that so?"

"Mm-hmm," she said, giving me the evil 'I'm onto you' look she specialized at, but I didn't let her win.

I shrugged. "Fine, whatever."

The strange thing was that when Silas saw that I was taking a break at a nearby table—what can I say, I wanted to be able to see him—he stood up with his coffee in hand and joined me. He actually sat at my table.

I was gobsmacked. "Hi.... um... Silas. Hello."

Silas flashed a soft smile. "Hello, Kai. Sorry to disturb you on your break."

"Oh, no, you're not. Definitely not. I was bored before you showed up. I mean, uh, I didn't have anything to— Hey, what's up?"

He chuckled, but at least he didn't seem to laugh at me, which I totally appreciated. "I talked to Wes, the owner of JustInk, and he said he would love to see your portfolio tonight. Are you free after seven?"

I looked at the clock. "I finish at six, so... yes. But I would have to go home and grab the folio, and I'm on my bike, so... yeah, I'll make it work."

"Or I can drive you," he shrugged, "if you want."

Wow, what a strange day. Silas was acting strange, smiling, looking at me in a sort of intense way, and telling me his friend would look at my silly little portfolio. *Oh my god, breathe, Kai.*

"Kai?"

"Fuck—fudge, sorry! Yeah, that works. I mean, you don't have to drive me, but if you don't mind driving me, then, yeah. Uh, thanks."

The corners of his eyes crinkled. "I don't mind. There's some time until then, so how about I pick you up after your shift ends, at six, did you say?"

"Yeah," I croaked. "Six."

He nodded and stood up. "I'll see you then."

Just like that, I had just had a conversation with my dream man, where he smiled at me and everything, and he was going to pick me up later. I was going to faint.

May cackled when I rejoined her. "So, by that panicked slash dazed look on your face, I take it you have a date?"

"No. He's taking me to his friend, the tattoo titan, to look at my portfolio after work. Did that really just happen?"

She shrugged. "I didn't hear the whole thing, but it seemed like a pretty convincing mirage. For your sake, I hope it happened."

"Gee, thanks," I quipped. "What would I do without you?"

"So..." she drew the word out as she gave me a once-over, "he's gonna pick you up looking like that?"

"Shut up and make your voodoo coffee."

She cackled. The witch. Honestly, though, I was in a pretty good mood after that. Considering I had a date—

I mean an appointment, or meeting, or whatever.

With the man of my fudging dreams.

***

SILAS

I am the first to admit when something is strange, but I refused to admit that helping a kid out was somehow bad. Kai was such a deserving person, and so talented, he deserved someone to take a chance on him. Even though Wes sounded strange on the phone, I refused to think about it.

Except I was thinking about it.

Not because I made this meeting happen, but because I offered to drive Kai. It just came out of my mouth. I saw a problem and solved it. That was all. Right?

Right.

The other problem was that when I went home to get ready for Kai, I changed my clothes twice and wondered why it even mattered what I was wearing since I was just driving the boy. It wasn't a date or anything.

I shook my head, dispelling the brain fart.

No, I was just doing a friend a favor, so I tried not to overthink it and did some work before the time came, then I went out to the car and drove to Starbucks, which took about ten minutes. When I entered the shop, Kai was there without his Starbucks apron or hat, just himself and his smile. I felt a strange tug in my stomach, but decided it was another blip.

He walked my way, his smile growing. "Hey, Silas."

"Hey, kid," I said, then frowned. He wasn't a kid, not really. He seemed to be in his twenties, so why did I say that?

It dimmed Kai's smile. "So... let's go?"

"Yes." I let him go first, then pointed at my car, which was a simple black Mazda.

"Fancy car you got there."

I laughed. "It's not fancy."

"Uh huh," he said as he got into the car and belted himself in, ginger in every movement as if he were afraid he'd break something. When I got in, he was looking around with a sense of amazement on his face. I wondered what he saw. There wasn't anything personal in the car. It was a sterile environment, really.

"So, the rest of the day was boring," he babbled as I drove off. His long skinny-jeans-clad leg was shaking up and down, not like he was nervous but like he was bursting with energy. His arms and fingers were just as skinny and long, delicate even. I imagined it helped with drawing. He kept talking. "There was this woman with a dog in her purse, and she kept calling it Princess Diana."

I snorted.

"I mean, that's as good a name as any, but I'm pretty sure I saw some male parts under all the fur. Man, was it furry down there."

I snorted again.

"Anyway, May got angry when the woman made her redo her order three times and threatened to curse her soul to the pits of hell. And believe me, if anyone could do it, May can." He shuddered. "So, that was fun."

"I know all about tricky clients who make you redo things endlessly."

"Oh, yeah?"

"Yes. I'm an architect, and this last project is really testing my patience. The client made me redo the whole design twice and then redo the garden, and I'm afraid the horror hasn't ended yet."

Kai laughed, a musical sound I wanted to hear more of. "Wow, no kidding. And here I thought you worked at a bank or something."

"You thought I was boring?"

"Oh my god, no. I didn't mean that. I thought you were interesting, actually. Fuck—I mean fudge. I just meant that you look like you work at a place where you have to wear fancy suits and shit—I mean stuff."

I laughed at the cursing-not-cursing thing. "Do you have younger siblings?"

"Uh, yeah, actually. Why do you ask?"

"The fudge and shoot thing kind of gave it away."

"Ha! Yeah. My mom had Johnny a couple of years back. When I went to visit, she said I should wash my mouth next time. So, I tried."

My GPS led us to the address Kai gave me. His place was a nondescript five-floor apartment building. I parked in front.

"Thanks! I'll just be a minute."

"No rush. Take your time," I said, regretting that I won't get to see his apartment. "I'll check my email."

"Okay," he said as he jumped out of the car, then rushed up the stairs. He went so fast, I blinked and he was gone.

When he came back ten minutes later, he looked better. He had changed his t-shirt to a button-down and smelled less like coffee and more like vanilla. He held a huge black folder of what I imagined were his designs. I was dying to see them.

"May I?" I asked.

His eyes went wide. "Oh, wow. I mean, yeah, okay." He shook his head and blushed that beautiful pink color as he gave me the folder.

I opened it and stared.

The first design was a woman with a snake tattoo around her arm. The details were so intricate, it looked almost real. There was a tongue and tail and everything. It made me shudder. The next was a man with barbed wire around his neck.

Jesus.

More and more designs, and more and more amazing talent, and I wondered how a ray of sunshine had such dark ideas.

I felt him shuffle next to me and I looked up. He was chewing his lip, probably worrying about what I thought. I hadn't said anything since I opened the folder. "Kai, these are incredible. The details are stunning. You are so talented, I'm... speechless."

He gave me a shy smile. "Really? Oh, wow. Thanks."

I chuckled. "Thank you for showing me. Wes is going to love these."

"Don't jinx it!" he said in horror.

Laughing and shaking my head, I gave him the folio back and drove off again, continuing our conversation.

"How did you get into drawing?" I asked.

He shrugged. "I've always just kind of done it."

"Did you study art?"

"No." He rubbed the folio and stared at it as a flush climbed up his neck, as if he were embarrassed to be the center of attention.

I didn't let that stop me. In fact, it egged me on. "Have you always wanted to do tattoo art?"

"Uh..." He pursed his lips in thought for a moment, and I caught myself staring.

Eyes on the road, Silas.

"Not really," Kai said. "I just got into it recently."

I could only imagine what else he'd drawn in the past if he was so good at this in a short amount of time.

I soon pulled into the small parking lot next to Wes's parlor, regretting that we didn't have more time to talk. "Here we are. JustInk."

"Wow, it looks great!"

I enjoyed Kai's enthusiasm. He was like a little ball of energy: always moving, talking, jumping around, and smiling. God, I wished I had someone like him in my life, which was a weird thought. Maybe another blip.

"Thanks for giving me a ride!"

I removed my seatbelt and said, "I'll go in with you if you don't mind. I have to ask Wes something after you guys finish, then I can drive you back."

"Oh, you don't have to do that."

"I want to," I blurted out, which shut Kai up.

We went in together and the familiar smells and sights of my best friend's workplace engulfed me.

Last time I was there, Ellie was with me.

Chapter 4

KAI

There was a young guy covered in tats and piercings at the front desk with a young face and curly, dark hair. He played with his lip piercing as he watched us walk toward him, then jutted his chin. "What up, Mr. G."

"Jesus, Matthew, you've been hard at work this year."

Matthew shrugged. "It's free, so... you know."

Silas nodded, but he was no longer smiling. I thought it was strange that he stopped when we came in, considering that it was his friend's workplace.

A beautiful, plump woman with green hair and even more tats came out of somewhere and looked at us. Her eyes went wide. "Silas, what are you—I mean, hi, how are you, you cheeky devil?"

Silas nodded at her, as well. "Hi Jazz, it's good to see you."

"It's been a long time, hasn't it? You could have called, you know. Asked about my kids, complained about work. You know, like friends do."

"Sorry, Jazz, I've been busy."

"Uh huh," she drolled, then hurried over to Silas and gave him a big hug. She was bigger than him but shorter, so he bent down to hug her back. She patted him on the back. "Good to see you."

"You too," Silas said, extricating himself from her and clearing his throat.

Jazz looked at him with sad eyes, which seemed unusual.

That's when she noticed I existed. "Hey, and who are you? Silas, did you bring your friend here to brand him? We've talked about that, and it's not cool."

Silas cleared his throat. "Very funny. How's your tramp stamp doing, by the way? Prince Harry, was it?"

"I look at him in the mirror every night, thank you very much. I just have to turn around a little and maybe lose a few pounds from here," she said, grabbing the left side of her butt.

I laughed at their conversation. This Jazz woman was hilarious.

"This is Kai," Silas said. "He brought his drawings for Wes to look at."

"Oh, that's great! You're a little artist, are you?"

It was funny how big she was and how small I was in comparison, but, at the same time, I liked it. Who cares about people's sizes, anyway? *Unless it's a guy you like*, I thought, *who is bigger than you and who can squeeze you and manhandle you and—shit, stop it!*

Not now, you moron, this is about art, not your dick.

"I heard a hyena and decided to check it out, but it's just Jazz laughing," someone said behind her, who I soon realized was Wes. He was taller than her, taller than everybody, really, and quite buff. He was the perfect daddy for some people I knew, but not for me. I liked them different.

"Hi, Kai," he said, smirking. "And my good-for-nothing best friend who didn't answer my call today, like I'm a used condom the morning after."

"Thank you for that image," Silas muttered. "You two go ahead and talk. I don't want to be in the way."

"Come on, Kai, follow me into the lion's den."

I smiled and followed him, leaving Silas behind. It was like leaving behind a favorite pair of jeans or the security blanket you take everywhere with you. He wasn't those things, but he could be.

If only he didn't think of me as a kid and saw me as someone who could give him what he needed.

***

SILAS

Anywhere I looked, there was Ellie. Laughing in the corner with Jazz, telling Matt he should wait until he was eighteen to get pierced, and joking with Wes about his new boy toy. Getting tattooed again, even though it was always hidden because her bosses were sticks in the mud. Her words, not mine.

"She's everywhere, isn't she?" Jazz sighed.

I turned to find her sitting on the couch, which was usually for customers, but there was no one there. Her smile was so sad.

"Yeah, she really is," I said.

I used to break down every time I saw something or heard something that reminded me of Ellie. Then, as time passed, I started to savor those things and feel both happy and sad, a strange mixture that tore up my insides but also stitched them back together.

I wanted to remember Ellie as lovely as she was before everything... happened.

Jazz patted the seat next to her. "Come here, honey, sit."

I sat.

"How are you? Working hard, as always? Any new flames?"

I snorted. "You're kidding."

Despite the sadness in her eyes, they met mine with a kindness I hadn't seen since… Ellie.

"No, I'm not," she said. "You forget she was my best friend. I knew her better than anyone. She would have wanted you to find happiness again. She would want you to find someone."

I shook my head. "There's no one. There's never going to be."

"Don't close your heart, honey. We never know what waits around the corner. For Ellie, just… keep your eyes wide open."

Shaking my head, I said, "Okay," to mollify her. It didn't mean I agreed with her. Once you've known what real love is, how does anything else compare? How does anyone else ever match up to what you had?

Ellie was perfect.

There are no other perfect people in this sad, gray world.

"Thanks a lot!" Kai beamed from the back. There was so much energy and cheer in his voice, I found myself smiling.

"There you go," Jazz whispered.

Ignoring her, I stood and greeted Wes and Kai as they returned to the lobby. Looking at them side by side, there was another weird tug in my stomach, but I was used to disregarding those around Kai. He was just the kind of person who brought out emotions in others, which wasn't a bad thing. It was just disconcerting for someone who was so used to feeling nothing.

"Are you kidding me?" Wes asked, looking straight at me. "All those months going to Starbucks, and you didn't know Kai here is a fucking savant?"

Kai chuckled as that familiar flush rose on his neck.

Jazz grinned. "Aww. So, you joining us, hun?"

"He is definitely joining us," Wes said as he slapped Kai on the back, almost knocking the boy over. "I'll work out the schedule and make sure he gets hours with everyone. We already fleshed out a loose schedule around his other job, but hopefully, in a few months, that won't be a problem anymore."

"Great," I said, proud of my boy. *No, not my boy.* Again, a blip.

Kai was practically vibrating with happiness, obviously trying to tone it down, which I knew because I'd seen him do it before around strangers. I wondered how much I'd actually noticed about him without knowing it.

"Thanks, Wes, really," Kai said. "I can't wait to start!"

Wes patted him on the shoulder, gentler this time. "Monday. Don't be late, or else."

"Don't scare the boy," I said. "And call me later."

Wes walked us out, giving me his annoying smirk again, like I was a teenager on a date or something. "I'm tired of talking to your voicemail. You call me."

I rolled my eyes. "Fine."

Kai and I went back to the car and hopped inside. He belted in and looked at me, grinning.

"I take it by your ridiculous smile it went well?"

His smile grew, if that were even possible. "It was the best! Oh my god, Wes' style is amazing. I showed him my stuff and he liked it, but his style is... whoa, out of this world. I can't wait to work with him."

Another weird pang. It didn't help that I knew what Wes' taste was: slim boys he could throw around and fuck. And, of course, he was a much better bet for Kai, seeing as I had nothing left to offer a person. Okay, now I was getting sick to my stomach, thinking about Wes and Kai together in bed.

I did this. It was my fault.

I remained silent for the rest of the drive and Kai didn't babble on this time. He just shook his leg up and down, drawing invisible patterns on the window.

When we reached his place, I tried to smile.

"Thanks, Silas," he said. "I really, really appreciate this."

"I'm glad I could help, Kai. You deserve all the best things."

His face went blank, perhaps confused by what I said. "Oh, thanks. Uh, see you tomorrow?"

I cocked my head.

"For your caramel macchiato, remember?"

I laughed. "Right, for my caramel macchiato. How could I forget?" I shook my head. "Have a good night, Kai. I'll see you tomorrow."

He flashed a sweet smile, looking at me through his lashes, and for the first time since Ellie, I felt like I wanted to kiss someone. *Fuck*.

Ignoring the unwelcome feeling, I watched him bounce out of the car and into his building.

I lingered there, staring at Kai's building for several long minutes, before driving back to my empty home.

***

KAI

"Oh my *god*," I said as I rushed through the front door. Jason was in his room, on his window ledge, smoking. I rushed over to his bed and sat down with a mighty bounce, and then a few more enthusiastic ones.

"Whoa," he said. "What's up? You're all bouncy."

"I went to JustInk and Wes, the owner, saw my designs and he liked them. He was so fudging amazing. We talked and we laughed and he said I could go back Monday and that they're gonna teach me. *Aah*!"

Jason laughed. "Holy shit. This is too much for me right now. I'm all mellow, and you're all jumping out of your skin and shit."

I kept bouncing anyway. "The other day, Silas sat at my table and said he could talk to his friend, and I guess he did, then he offered to drive me and waited for me, and he drove here like twice today, and he's so nice, and his smile is so nice, and... gah! I wanted to kiss him!"

"Why didn't you?"

I deflated. "Because he thinks I'm a kid, remember? He doesn't act like he wants anything other than friendship, so..." I shrugged.

"Right. Well, give it time, then."

"Don't say that. When people say that, it means it's never going to happen and you've wasted your life pining over someone." I crashed on his bed, my hands over my face. "I hate this. Why does he have to be nice on top of hot and handsome and mysterious and brooding and hot?"

"You said hot twice."

"That's how hot he is," I said, sitting up on the bed. "So, that's me, pathetic little Kai who likes the losers, the straight men, the phobes, and also apparently the nice guys who think I'm a kid."

"Stop being so melodramatic. Come try this."

"No, thanks," I said and started to leave. "Remind me that I'm stupid tomorrow, okay? I don't want to set an alarm just for that."

Jason guffawed. "You got it, skinny man."

Back in my room, I put away my portfolio and sat on the bed, thinking about how amazing it was that I would finally do something with my art. I didn't want to get my hopes up too high, but still, this was progress. I was going to rock this apprenticeship thing, or at least, I would try my best.

God, I hope it's not like... super hard. Or what if I see the blood and faint at the sight? No, Kai, calm down, you'll do fine.

To distract myself from crazy thoughts and potential future meltdowns, I opened the Geeklandia forums and my messages. Simon had ranted on and on about the difference between high fantasy and modern fantasy, then, surprisingly, mentioned he might visit the States.

What the...?

Oh, wow, I typed. *That's cool. So, we can maybe meet up, huh? I bet there will be a monster clash between the titans of sci-fi and fantasy.*

He typed back, *Watch out, mere mortals! We're going to obliterate everything in a five-mile radius. Hell, make it ten miles.*

I laughed. *It's gonna be epic. Okay, I had a long day, so I gotta go to bed. Make sure you watch the episode with the Halloween apocalypse.*

He typed back, *Night night, sleeping beauty.*

I closed the laptop, went to the kitchen, and whipped up some pasta, which I ate in two minutes, almost choking. Then, I was ready to head to bed. It was only ten pm, but after the day I'd had, I was ready to snooze out.

Chapter 5

KAI

The next day, I was in such a good mood that it freaked out May. During a lull around noon, she gave me a strange look and said, "Don't tell me: Your dream man kissed you."

I rolled my eyes. "No. I'm going to study under Wes at JustInk!"

"*Under* him, huh? That's the tat god? Good for you!"

"I mean he's going to mentor me, you hag. There's nothing weird between us, okay? He's just Silas' friend and my new mentor."

"That's how some romcoms start."

"Not the gay ones," I deadpanned, making her laugh. "Besides, I told you, Wes is not really my type."

"A god is not your type? Honey, what happened to you? Did you fall on your head as a child? Was your dad one of those distracted professor types?"

I glared at her. "What does my dad have to do with anything?"

"Oh, trust me, it's the deciding factor," she said as she looked at something on her phone. "And, by the way, I am looking for the best love spells for you, just in case you need it. You're welcome."

"Oh, my god. Don't even joke about that."

She turned her phone so I could see she wasn't actually kidding. I covered the screen with my hand and said, "If you put bad juju on my life, I will defriend you on every social media platform."

"*Ooh*, I'm shaking in my ballet slippers."

Someone cleared their throat, making me jump. I was behind the muffin stand and didn't see the stranger approach. May looked at the man, arching an unimpressed eyebrow while I emerged from my hiding spot and asked, "Welcome to Starbucks. What can I get you today?"

The man looked at me like I was a bug on his watch. Seriously weird. He was tall, dressed in some kind of regal coat that went down to his knees, and had the kind of haircut you know cost hundreds of dollars. His watch alone probably cost more than a car. He was good-looking, but severe. Also, he seemed impatient.

"English tea," he said, sounding bored.

"Right away," I replied, then gave May a brief glance. "That'll be..."

He threw a twenty-dollar bill on the counter and said, "Keep the change, you need it," then moved on like nothing interesting had happened.

I just stood there, blinking like an idiot. *Who is this jerk?* We got those occasionally, like any business, but this man was a serious asshole, looking at people like they were a lower organism or something. It ticked me off.

But as always, I kept smiling. This was work.

Five minutes later, my smile grew as Silas walked through the door. When he saw me, he smiled back and came straight to the till, greeting me while I cheerfully yelled his order to May without him asking for it. He seemed to be amused and somehow softer than usual. Sometimes, he looked like he was somewhere else mentally, but he was *there* that day.

There with me.

"Silas," the jerk asshole said from a table at the other end of the café. His voice was loud and firm. Commanding.

Silas turned to the source and frowned, then sighed, then turned to me and nodded. Weird. He went to the jerk asshole and sat next to him at the table.

Fudge!

"Oh, no, he did not," May said, incensed. "Please don't tell me your man is friends with that shit head."

"He's not my man," I muttered. "And, I hope not?"

"Holy goddess, there's no accounting for taste, is there?"

I thought about May's comment as I stared at Silas and the jerkface. My head filled with all kinds of awful questions. Were they on a date? Was that the kind of man Silas liked, if he even was gay? Were they friends?

Hiding behind the muffin stand, I cursed the fact that I couldn't eavesdrop, but then realized I was being crazy again. Silas wasn't mine.

If anything, he was my friend. Even that was a stretch. He was a customer who did me one favor. It's not like we were hanging out together.

With nothing else to do and those burning, stupid questions in my head, I kept working, but I glanced their way from time to time.

I couldn't help it.

***

SILAS

How could Nathaniel Mars take the one good thing in my life, my visits with Kai, and turn it into a shitshow?

I sat there as he explained something about the garden and showed me my prints on his iPad. The hedges in the northeast corner were too high. The fountain wasn't high enough. Tiny little details that he could have discussed with the dozen other people who worked on his fucking garden. Or at least over the phone.

And why did he have to come here, of all places?

"So, you can come tomorrow and take a look? Joe said he can show you some possible solutions."

"I can talk with Joe on the phone," I said, constantly turning toward Kai because watching him work calmed me down. I did not want to explode all over Future and Past Designs' biggest fucking client in the last decade.

"What are you looking at?"

"Nothing," I muttered. "I'm going to get a muffin. You want anything?"

"No, thank you."

I didn't waste time and headed for the muffin stand, pretending to consider my options—other than the option of chewing my client's head off. God, this was easier a few months ago when I didn't give a fuck about the tiny changes or the weird things clients requested or all the other little inconsistencies that happened when working with people.

How was I so much better at this then? I feel like barbed wire.

"Do you want a muffin or something?" Kai whispered, breaking through my mutinous thoughts. It looked like he was hiding back there, or like he was conferring with a fellow spy about a mission.

I laughed, shaking my head. "What are you doing back there? Aren't you supposed to be the face of this place?"

"Nah, May is the face, but sometimes she gets pissy and I hide out here on account of her wicked skills with eye of newt and tarantula legs."

I blinked. "What?"

"Sorry," he said, laughing. "She's a witch. It's, uh, what she does. You know, like spells and shit—I mean stuff."

"Wow. Does she charge for it?"

Kai burst out laughing, turning heads, one of which was May's. When she saw me, she waved like we actually knew each other. I waved back.

"That's her 'I'm gonna put a spell on you' wave," Kai said, his tone so casual he might as well have been remarking on the weather.

I squinted at him. "You're joking."

"I'm totally joking. Although, she *does* have a wave like that, but this wasn't that particular wave."

I laughed again, struck that Kai made me laugh twice in one brief conversation. Laughter that usually happened once in months. It was amazing how happy and open he was, how ready to have a quick laugh, how—unbeknownst to him—he healed broken hearts one smile at a time.

The boy was an angel.

"So, do you want a muffin, or do you just want to start a staring contest?" he asked, smirking. He also bit his lip, making me feel unbidden urges.

More blips.

I sighed, tired of ignoring those. Maybe I should have accepted that they only happened around Kai and embraced them? With that in mind, I asked, "When do you finish your shift?"

"Oh, uh..." he stumbled, looking up at the clock. "Two o'clock?"

"Do you want to do something later?"

His eyes went so big, it was amusing. "With—with you?"

"That's the idea. I mean, you probably have plans—"

"No, no plans. No plans here, nope. You can check the definition of a plan in the dictionary, and you won't find me there."

"Okay," I said. "See you later, then."

He nodded, looking a bit dazed, and as I headed back to the odious creature at the corner table, I wondered what in the world I had just done.

Nathaniel was looking at his phone, tapping on something or other. When he looked up, he frowned at me. "Took you long enough," he muttered, putting his phone down. "Where's your muffin?"

"I forgot, I guess," I said, but didn't elaborate.

Armed with Kai's smile and his easy jokes, I spent the rest of Nathaniel's 'visit' with a clear head and almost a smile on my face.

***

KAI

May was glaring at me because I kept messing up orders. She had to leave the register and take over the machine, even though it was my turn to make the drinks.

"You're vibrating," she hissed. "Stop it."

I couldn't help it. In just a few minutes, I would 'do something' with Silas, whatever that meant. He probably meant it as a friend thing, but my mind was turning it into a sexy thing. Definitely sexy things.

I wanted to do sexy things with Silas. A lot.

He was so solid, and I could imagine him without clothes on, and I was pretty sure I would like anything he hid under there. Even a dad bod. I would fudging love that. Plus, I never really liked the buff guys anyway; I prefer a body that's more natural. The deciding factor of hotness for me was that he was strong, and I could tell that he was. Silas was bigger than me, twice as big—taller, wider, and just... solid. I loved that. It made me drool.

So I continued to vibrate like an idiot.

"Ugh!" May said. "Stop, just go take a break."

"But my shift is over soon."

"I don't care. Go make yourself pretty or whatever. I can't work with you like this. And you better fuck up on your date because if you do this to me again tomorrow, I will curse you. *Literally*."

I shuddered. "Sorry."

"Go," she ordered, then winked, letting me know she wasn't really mad, just annoyed at my exaggerated enthusiasm.

Sometimes, people found me tiring, which I couldn't fix because I am who I am. Some would say I should tone it down. I can lessen it somewhat, but really, how can someone change who they are? They can't, so they don't.

I like being excited about things, damn it. It's fun.

There were ten minutes left until the date, or whatever it was, so I went in the back and cleaned myself up a little, using the change of clothes I have just in case I splashed coffee on myself or something. I probably still smelled like coffee beans and looked like I was high on methamphetamines. When I came out of the employee door and back into the café, Silas was there, waiting.

He took one look at me and smiled.

He *smiled*, like fully smiled. Like I'd never seen him smile before, and it was a bit... dazzling, blinding, disconcerting, lovely? Perfect.

"Hey," I breathed. "Hi."

"Hi, Kai," he said. "Should I wave to May again, or will she turn me into a toad if I even try?"

"You can wave to her."

He waved at May, whose annoyed face broke into an exasperated smile and a wave off.

"Did something happen?" he asked.

"I just kind of annoyed her to death, but I'm hoping she's used to it by now."

"I can't imagine you annoying anyone," Silas said. When I looked at his face, he was so painfully genuine I didn't know what to make of it.

***

SILAS

Ellie died three years ago. Since then, I had not been on a date. Not that I considered my outing with Kai a date, exactly, but it was an outing with a new friend, which kind of felt like a date.

I felt stilted and out of practice, but I tried to get out of my head and experience whatever this was. To experience Kai.

We walked down Main Street, talking about anything and everything under the sun. He told me where he was from, about his family, about the small town he grew up in, and about his favorite TV show, which I'd never seen, but thought I could give it a try later.

I didn't give much in return simply because I was happier to listen to him. Besides, my stories weren't as happy as his were. I didn't want to ruin the mood by mentioning my dead wife. I just stayed in the safe zone of work, friends, and books I liked. When I didn't want to answer something, I asked him a question, and he always had funny answers.

"Yeah, I live with a couple of guys. One is a major player, but he's straight, and the other one is a sort of a junkie, but mostly weed. Anyway, if you ever hear porno being made, it's probably

Parker, and if you ever smell marijuana that's altogether too strong for any human being, it's probably Jason."

I laughed at his descriptions.

"Oh my god," he said, looking at me with a horrified expression. "I didn't mean that our apartment is some kind of criminal den! Fudge, that sounded bad. I swear, I don't smoke the stuff and I don't feature in porn."

I laughed harder. Tears actually fell. "God," I panted, "Kai, you're insane. I wasn't going to send the police to your address, you know. You can relax."

He relaxed and laughed, though he still seemed nervous. "Sorry. I'm so fudging awkward. This is weird for me because I haven't been on a date in forever." He stopped walking.

I stopped as well, turning to see why he stopped.

"I mean, shit—shoot. Fuck—fudge! I mean... it's not a date. Obviously. Right? Right. I'm sorry, can you just push the off button on that handy Kai remote you got over there?"

I couldn't laugh anymore. My stomach hurt, so I just held him by the shoulders and squeezed him. "Kai, can you please stop making me laugh so hard for a minute? Otherwise, we'll have to call an ambulance."

He'd flushed pink up to the tops of his ears. So adorable.

To be honest, it felt like a date and it probably was a date, but I couldn't say it out loud... because of Ellie. Instead, I flashed him a reassuring smile and said, "Let's go find something fun to do."

We ended up going down to the pier and tried every stupid fun thing we saw there—the bumpy cars, which I'd never tried, the pendulum ride, which Kai had never tried, and so on. We ate fried corn, caramel apples, and cotton candy. While Kai was probably fine, my stomach hated me after that. We watched people enjoying their Sunday afternoon with their families and I tried not to think about Ellie. For the first time in three years,

I succeeded. I focused all my attention on the bouncy boy next to me.

Kai was a force of nature. He wanted to try everything, do everything, and go everywhere, and I followed suit because his enthusiasm was contagious. He was like a pulsing ball of light that transformed everything it touched.

When darkness descended and it was time to say good night, I looked into his eyes and tried to imagine what it would be like if I could kiss him. If I could be with him. If this could be our regular Sunday ritual. If he could be mine and I could be his. Like everything, however, this dream had to end, as well. It was an illusion we had for a day, and it was nice, but it was just a wish whispered by a person who lost his soulmate.

I could not replace Ellie. I wouldn't.

After finally saying good night to Kai, I went home on numb feet, stumbled into the bathroom, and threw up everything in my stomach.

Chapter 6

SILAS

It wasn't the alarm that woke me up, it was the stupid door shaking.

"I know you can hear me, you lousy fucker. Open the door!" someone bellowed. After some more muttering and a jingling of keys, the door opened and Wes appeared, looking furious. When he saw how pathetic I looked cuddled up on the sofa, with my clothes still on, the duvet on top of me, and all the pillows scattered about, he let out a deep sigh.

Without another word, he went to the kitchen, followed by the sounds of rummaging through cabinets, then running water. Probably to make coffee.

I felt a pang of regret since I'd been so good recently. I hadn't had a meltdown for a while, and Wes had probably thought he wouldn't have to come to my rescue. Yet, here we were, again. The man was a saint.

He brought me coffee and a Pop Tart. I looked at them like they personally offended me with their existence. Then, I looked at Wes, who was running his hand through his hair, avoiding my eyes, and huffing like he was that wolf who wanted to bring down the piggys' house.

"So, Sara called," he said. "Said you were MIA."

Of course my assistant called him. She did it a few other times in the past, but not recently.

"Sorry," I muttered as I took the coffee in my hands, trying to feel some warmth, but it was just a stupid mug with stupid liquid in it. It burned going down, which was a relief. At least I could still feel *something*.

"Did something happen?" he asked.

What was I supposed to say? I couldn't kick him out because he was the only true friend I had left. Everyone else got tired of me and my grief. I couldn't tell him the truth because it was too difficult... or could I?

"Is it about Ellie?" he asked. At least he didn't act like I was mental for still grieving for my dead wife. At least he sounded genuine when he asked or said her name.

"What else can it be about?" I snapped, so tired of feeling nothing, then feeling everything at once.

He nodded. "Okay. Tell me about it?"

I had a terrible feeling tears were welling up in my eyes, even though I had expressly forbidden them from doing that. "I feel so... guilty." There it was.

"Why do you feel guilty, my friend?"

"Because Ellie's gone. The most wonderful person in the world is gone, and last night, I spent time with someone else who is also wonderful, but how can I even... how can I even think about that? I can't replace her, Wes. I won't fucking do it. I can't." My whole body was shaking, and the forbidden tears rolled down my cheeks.

Wes sat next to me on the sofa and rubbed my back while I shook and sobbed like an idiot. I thought I'd cried all the tears and that I was running on empty. Apparently, embarrassingly, I had more stored up.

Wes was patient as he waited for me to get it out of my system.

"I can't, I can't..." I repeated, refusing to imagine a world without Ellie and me in it. A world without her carefree laughter, her amazing heart, and her weird love of spicy food. Without her delicate hands, her soft lips, and her bright eyes.

I held on to the memories of looking into her eyes, kissing her lips, and of our hands woven together a thousand times.

Crying like that felt like purging, like something had stuck in my throat and I needed to gag endlessly to get it out. When I finally did, I felt lighter and calmer than I had in a long time.

Mostly, I still felt like a lousy cheater.

I laughed ruefully. "Fuck, I'm sorry, Wes. I don't know what came over me. I just needed to let it out, I guess."

"Does this have anything to do with Kai?"

I shook my head. "No, of course not. Nothing to do with him. We're just—" I was tired of lying to myself, and Wes didn't deserve for me to lie to him. "Yes, it does. I went out with him yesterday."

"You had a date?"

I kept shaking my head, wanting to deny it. "I think... maybe?"

Wes chuckled. "You couldn't tell?"

I sniffed and blew my nose, getting rid of the last vestiges of my meltdown, knowing that another might always lurk around the corner. This was so exhausting. Some days, I just wanted to give up.

I shrugged. "I don't know. I was at Starbucks, looking at him, and he was so happy, so vibrant. I guess... I wanted that, so I asked if he wanted to do something after work. He said yes, then we went to the pier and did a million things together. It was... nice."

"Sounds like a date to me," Wes said, smiling. "Don't you think after everything, you deserve a bit of happiness?"

"I'm fine. I have my work and your annoying ass. What else do I need?"

"You need to feel alive again," Wes asserted, making me meet his eyes. "You need to rejoin the world of the living. You need to let something make you feel alive again. From everything I've seen so far, I think we both know that could be Kai."

"No. He's a healthy young man who needs more than…" I waved my hand at myself, "this. More than this mess. It's not just about Ellie. He doesn't need someone who's already half dead, who can give him less than he deserves."

"Silas, you have the biggest heart in the world, and I know it's big enough to love two people. Even more than two. You don't have to replace one with the other, just love both of them."

"Don't you think that's selfish?" I asked.

"Why don't you let the boy decide what he wants, huh? You can't make decisions for other people, Silas."

"What about Ellie? Is she just a footnote in this story?" I asked, feeling indescribable anger and sadness mixed together to make something unbearably heavy in my chest.

"No, she isn't. Neither are you. Neither is Kai," Wes said. "You found the love of your life at twenty, and that's so fucking lucky, but when that person goes, you have to keep living. Take that energy and give it to someone else, because it needs to be shared. Give it to Kai. At least try."

"When did you become Yoda?"

"Shut the fuck up. That wrinkled little green guy has nothing on me, man. The truth I speak, you know. And see soon, we all shall."

I burst out laughing. "Jesus, you're such a geek."

"A geek who knows what's what, my friend, and who knows your ungrateful ass better than you know yourself."

"I'm sorry, but that sounded awfully gay."

He guffawed. "There we go, that's better. Now, let's pretend this meltdown was just a hiccup and plunge on through, shall we?"

I nodded, trying to convince myself he was right. It had been three years since I wanted to feel something for someone.

Maybe I could at least try.

***

KAI

Silas didn't come for his flat white the day after our outing. He always came, every day, even if it was just once, and he never missed a day. But then... it was almost time to go to JustInk, and instead of excitement, I felt... confused, disappointed, worried, and a bunch of other things I did not want to feel.

The day before at the pier was a dream—the perfect date I could ever imagine with someone. I thought we had so much fun. We laughed and talked so much, and by the end, I was certain it was, in fact, a date.

Then the end came and he looked at me in this sort of sad way, like he was letting me go for some reason.

I didn't understand it.

There was no kiss, not even on the cheek, just a quiet 'good night,' then he walked away into the dark, out of sight, but never out of mind.

When I got home, I decided that maybe I'd imagined the whole thing. Maybe it was just friends going out. Or maybe it had been a date, but for some reason, Silas decided not to kiss me. I tossed and turned most of the night, confused and overanalyzing every little thing to no avail.

I had no idea what happened.

The next day, I was cranky, making mistakes again, annoying May, writing the wrong names on cups, and looking around, hoping he would show up.

Pathetic.

Finally, when the time came to leave, May breathed a sigh of relief and waved me off, muttering 'good luck' as an afterthought.

I headed to JustInk on my bike and managed to get there with ten minutes to spare. Inside, there was one girl waiting on the couch, smiling, and that Matthew guy at the front desk, looking at his phone. He glanced up and nodded, then went back to his phone, so I just hung out for a few minutes, not wanting to interrupt anyone in case they were working.

"Where is my new apprentice?" someone called, and Wes poked his head out, smiling at me. "There you are. I have bought you a red and green uniform and a yellow cape. You are to wear them as you perform your duties."

I stared at him.

He burst out laughing. "Aww, man, I love it when they're so easy." He winked. "Okay, come on, Kai, follow me into the wolf's den."

"It was the lion's den before."

"Lion, wolf, all predators, so it's technically still correct. Just don't call it the weasel's den or the owl's den or something; that would be just awful."

I laughed at his chipper mood and decided to just go with it and kill any thoughts I had about Silas. This was my chance to do my art. Finally.

He took me through the curtain, down a short hallway, and into a bigger space with two partitions. He said someone was always working, but not more than two at a time. He said he usually liked to work alone, that Jazz didn't have any preference, and that the new guy was still on probation after having someone pass out on him.

He showed me all the gear: the power supply, the tattoo gun, how to mount the needles, all the different types of needles, and how to use it all properly. He stressed more than anything being sanitary: washing my hands before doing anything, using gloves, covering almost everything in fresh plastic wrap, *always* using new needles, and *never* dipping right into a pot of ink instead of using the little plastic cups. He later demonstrated on a living person—that girl who had been waiting on the sofa. She didn't seem to mind having an audience; she smiled and watched as the needles pierced her skin repeatedly.

Later, Wes explained, "You have some people who are squeamish, so they won't look at it while you work. Others are morbidly curious or just enjoy watching the process, and even some who enjoy the pain—usually for the endorphin rush. You might even get someone who doesn't like blood, but for some reason, they decided they have to have a tattoo. This is why we give them a questionnaire to start with, plus all the legal mumbo-jumbo, so if they answer something in a way that should make you pause, you follow up."

I nodded. I wished I was taking notes, but then again, I'd always had good memory and Wes said I would learn by observing him, then by practicing. This wasn't like school.

The final thing he asked of me was to practice tattooing on a banana. He said it was similar to human skin and would help me get used to it. "Let's just nip any fear or nerves in the bud. I want you to be comfortable with this from day one," he explained as he made sure I was holding the machine properly, explaining what to avoid if I wanted to keep all my fingers. Finally, he turned it on.

Man, what a rush it was.

Obviously, the result was ugly and unfocused, but he said that the more I practiced, the better I'd become. "Try to come in after work every day if you can, at least for an hour, so you can get some consistent practice. That's the only way you'll get good enough to graduate from bananas to people."

I laughed as I stared down at the desecrated fruit. "Oh, I will. I promise."

"So," he said when we were done and walking down the hallway to the waiting area. "Heard you had a date yesterday?"

I tripped over my feet and slammed against the wall. "Fudge."

Wes laughed and righted me. "Sorry, didn't mean to startle you."

"No, that's okay," I said. "I mean, it's fine, it's nothing. I mean, Silas and I went to the pier. There was the bumpy rides and cotton candy, lots of it. Caramel apples. People watching. That puke-inducing thing that spins in the air. It was fun."

What was I even saying?

He chuckled. "Good, I'm glad. Silas needs to get out more." He put a hand on my shoulder. "But just so you know, I will disembowel you with my instrument if you hurt that man in any shape or form."

I gaped at him. *Oh, fudge.*

He slapped me on the back, almost knocking me over like the first time, but he was laughing. "Don't worry. I'm sure Silas is perfectly capable of fucking things up himself, given half the chance."

What was even happening?

"Uh... okay?" Silas told his friend about the date? Had he said it was a date, or did Wes just assume? Did they talk today? Why hadn't he come to the café? Wes was in a good mood, so maybe Silas also was?

I was confused again.

"Hey, good job today. I'll see ya tomorrow, yeah?"

"Yes, yeah," I mumbled as he chuckled and winked at me, then walked back into his den. I stood dumbfounded in the waiting area, with Matthew glaring at me. "Hey, Matthew," I said, but he rolled his eyes and looked away.

Okay, then.

Jazz wasn't there, and they were getting ready to close, so I went outside, found my bike, and rode home, all the while wondering what happened with Silas and why it felt like I was missing a part of the puzzle.

Something didn't add up.

Chapter 7

SILAS

On Tuesday, I decided to go back to things as usual. There were some missed calls by Nathaniel Mars, which I chose to leave for later, but other than that, nobody at work had missed me. Sara had told people I was sick. No big deal.

The thing I was nervous about was seeing Kai.

It didn't make any sense because I always loved seeing him. He was the highlight of my days, but now that we'd had our sort-of-date, I wasn't sure how to act around him. So, I did my best not to think too much about it and jumped into the deep end, meaning going to Starbucks. It was lunchtime, so there were some people, but not as many as in the afternoon or the morning. There was breathing space. Talking space.

Kai was making drinks while May was on the register. When she saw me, she reacted a little, but seemed to shutter it.

Feeling nervous, I walked over and said, "Dark chocolate mocha, please."

Kai jumped and turned around to look at me with a shy smile. "Hey."

"Hi," I said, smiling back.

May cleared her throat and Kai went back to making the drinks. He had a couple more people waiting, and maybe then I'd be able to talk to him.

I waited for my drink, watching him work. Those long, deft fingers. That fluid, lean body. Those big blue eyes when they rose to meet mine. Beautiful.

"Here you go," he mumbled, looking at me from under his lashes. Fuck, was the boy doing it on purpose, trying to kill me?

"Thanks," I muttered, then went to find a table and calm down a little. I realized that after the conversation with Wes the day before, I uncorked something I had been keeping down this whole time. When I looked at Kai, I felt... things.

I felt flustered because I wanted to touch him, annoyed because I couldn't, and excited at the possibility he might let me. Overall, I was a mess.

So I called Wes.

"Yoda two-point-oh, how can I of service be to thee?"

"Stop," I said, laughing. "That was horrible. You're actually getting worse every time you try."

"'Do or do not. There is no try.'"

I cleared my throat. "So, how are things at JustInk? Has your new guy maimed anyone yet today?"

"Nah, unless you consider Kai the new guy, in which case he maimed a banana yesterday, but I forgave him."

"Of course he did. The banana must have been naughty."

"Listen to you trying to joke and shit. It's like watching a baby gazelle trying to walk, or a baby hedgehog trying to dig. It's cute."

"Fuck off," I groused.

"Kai was really good, by the way. I'm sensing a natural." He paused for a moment. "Is that why you called, you bastard? Of course it wouldn't be to ask me how I am, but to ask whether your new boy toy is performing."

"Don't say performing."

He cackled. "I made him put the needle down, get on his knees, open his mouth and take—"

"Stop it," I growled. "I will punch you."

He cackled some more. "I love it. Now I can finally tease you like a normal person. Hey, how about a threesome?"

"Goodbye," I said, hanging up. It was good to have my old friend back. Sometimes he got sad and looked at me like I was gone, and sometimes he looked worried I would do something stupid like hurt myself, and sometimes he just looked annoyed that he didn't have his friend to banter with.

I was glad to have him back, or maybe it would be more accurate to say I was glad to be back.

"Chocolate chip muffin for you and sprinkles for me," someone said, and I looked up to see Kai smiling as he sat down at my table.

"Aren't you supposed to be working?"

He shrugged. "May said it's okay because I don't have my head screwed on straight, whatever that means. Doesn't sound very gay at all."

I laughed. "No, it doesn't."

He bit his lip, like he wanted to say something.

"What is it, Kai?" I asked.

"Can I ask... are you, uh... you know, gay?" he muttered the last part, going silent and watching me like he was afraid I'd get mad or something.

I put my muffin down. "Well, technically, I am bisexual. What about you?"

Some pink colored his cheeks, making me want to kiss the fuck out of him, but obviously it couldn't happen there. Jesus, we were in public.

"I am. Gay, that is," he said. "Always have been."

"When did you know?"

He shrugged. "I always knew, but I guess maybe it was when I proclaimed that I was going to marry Heath Ledger when I was ten."

"Heath Ledger? Really?"

"He was the shit back in middle school. Then my mom said, 'okay then,' and went back to cooking, and that was the big reveal."

I enjoyed how much more relaxed Kai seemed after I shared my truth with him. He was still at that age where sharing your sexual preference was awkward, sometimes even dangerous. Since he was so small, I shuddered to think what kind of reactions he received in the past to make him so wary.

Wanting to put him further at ease, I said, "I was a late bloomer, myself. In high school, I knew for sure, even though I suspected before that. I was the typical jock who was supposed to flirt with the cheerleaders, and sometimes I did, but I also stole glances at the quarterback. It wasn't ideal."

Kai leaned over the table. "What happened?"

Having his full attention was a wonderful, heady feeling. I wanted to keep it on me for as long as I could, which was uncomfortable, but at least I wasn't denying myself or holding back anymore.

"I made a mistake, people found out, and we had to move towns."

"Ouch!" he said. "That sucks."

I shrugged. "You know, every experience carries a lesson with it. In that instance, I learned not to push anyone into something they weren't ready for. But I didn't get to use that lesson because a few months later I found—"

I stopped talking.

"You found what?" he asked.

Deciding on a half-truth, I said, "I found a girl I fell in love with, and we spent a lot of our young adult years together."

His eyebrows went up. "What happened with her? I mean, are you still...?"

"No," I said, focusing on my muffin. "No, and I haven't met anyone else since then."

Kai nodded, looking down at his muffin.

"I mean, I *hadn't*," I corrected, wondering if I should clarify, but I was saved by May, who called Kai back to work.

"Sorry," he said. "The witch calls."

I laughed. "Sure, no problem. See you later?"

"Yeah, of course." He flashed a broad, bright smile and gave me one of his shy under-the-eyelashes looks that I was getting dangerously attached to.

I was going to have to come back later.

***

KAI

"Hey, moony boy," May said. "Did you give that cup to that man over there?"

"Uh, yeah..."

She sighed. "Go get it back. This one is for him."

"Oh. Sorry."

She rolled her eyes, but at least she didn't huff and puff. She just smirked at me as I tried to focus on work while I was actually thinking about Silas.

I was thinking about how he came in today and looked at me so intensely, something he had never done before. He looked at my mouth and licked his lips, making me crazy, and he didn't seem to want to let me go.

I was no better.

I loved talking to him and peeling back his layers and learning what made him tick. I even enjoyed teasing him a little because

I could tell he liked it when I looked at him under my eyelashes. It was such a cheesy trick, but it worked!

So...

"Okay," May said when there was a lull. "Now, spill."

"What?"

"What's with the moony eyes and secret smiles? I'm half expecting you to sigh and start fanning yourself like a damsel in a period film."

"Stop," I muttered. "I am a man."

"You're a boy. A very cute boy, mind you, which is probably why a certain man has been coming here every day for the past, I don't know, year."

I rolled my eyes. "It's more like six months."

"Aww, you're counting. Now that you have that down to a tee, you can write those pesky wedding vows I've been hounding you about."

"Shut up, witch."

"Mm-hmm. So, what did you guys talk about? Is there going to be another date? Should I expect grandchildren?"

I laughed. "God, I don't know, and definitely *no* on the grandkids. You think I would give you anything to care for? You'd probably forget to feed it and turn it into a zombie vampire and add it to your undead army."

"It's a good idea, but... I don't know. Zombie vampire is a bit redundant. Maybe just a vampire; they're always in fashion, while zombies come and go."

I bit my lip, thinking about Silas and how he always smelled so good if I managed to lean a little and sniff without him noticing—like mint and musk and spice. Not like coffee.

"I've lost you to the fairies," May said, sighing. "Please remember me when you have a fabulous boyfriend and a fabulous life, and you don't need my love spells anymore. I will always think of you fondly as my first child out of wedlock."

Before we could continue the completely pointless conversation, someone entered the shop, making us look up. It was a guy somewhere around my age, taller than me, with dark hair, dark eyes, and glasses. He looked right at me and flashed a goofy smile.

I frowned. Did I know him?

"Welcome to Starbucks. What can I get you?" May asked.

The guy, however, did not look away from me, and his smile grew. "Hiya," he said, then cleared his throat. "Can you recommend anything?"

He had a British accent.

"Oh," I mumbled. "Sure..." I looked at the menu on the wall, then to the machine, and just shrugged. "You could get the drink of the day: the white chocolate mocha. It's a bit sweet, but does the trick."

"All right, cheers," the guy said with glee.

All right, then.

I made the drink while May charged him. She seemed to examine him closely, like she was sniffing something out, the way only she can. I still had no idea who the guy was.

"What's your name?" May asked.

"Simon," he said, and I almost dropped the cup. Now, I've written a lot of Simons on cups throughout my career, but this time I connected the dots, still disbelieving.

I turned to look at him. "Sim? Is that you?"

He clapped his hands. "Took you long enough, you bugger. Come here."

In a daze, I walked out from behind the counter and hugged him. I mean, this was the person I had talked to almost every day for months, and now he was here. I finally put a face to the name. *Wow!*

He laughed and squeezed me, picking me up in the air.

***

SILAS

It took me about five hours to finish every outstanding task from the previous day and update my calendar. Everything was going slow. I had to pitch one new project, but primarily, I was talking to Joe about Nathaniel Mars' estate, mostly about his garden. Joe laughed when I recounted what the man told me and that I said Joe was perfectly capable of figuring out the height of hedges.

After I finished up, I let Sara go home early and headed back to my favorite place, or where my favorite person was at the moment.

What I found when I arrived didn't compute with my expectation, but isn't that what always happens? I'd forgotten how life throws curveballs when you expect things to go smoothly.

I peeked through the glass and saw a tall guy embracing Kai in a very familiar manner, even picking him up off the ground. They appeared to be laughing. Now, I'm not normally a jealous guy, but this display felt... more than friendly. The guy was holding Kai's hands while they talked, then they sat on a couple of chairs, babbling on and laughing. The guy kept touching Kai.

I knew what it looked like: Like I had competition.

This could be the moment where I was the wiser, older guy and stepped aside to let Kai find someone who was better for him. Unfortunately, my body decided that it should rush to the guy it wanted and bulldoze everyone in its path.

The little bell jingled. Kai looked up, saw me, and smiled.

"Kai," I said, going directly to him. "Have you finished early?"

He blinked. "Oh shit—I mean shoot." He looked over to May.

"Don't worry," she said, waving her hand.

He looked back at me. "Sorry, did we have a date? I mean, fudge, you know what I mean," he babbled, then seemed to remember his friend was still there. "Holy shit—shoot—sorry. This is Simon. He's from London."

This Simon guy frowned at me, giving me a once-over, as I did the same to him. We both seemed to be sizing up the competition.

"Hi," he said, his tone curt.

"Hello." I reflected his tone.

"Uh," Kai stuttered, adorably confused, watching us. "This is Silas, my, uh, friend. He's an architect. Well, and his friend is this giant tatted-up guy who tattoos people for a living and who is currently mentoring me. Kind of sounds confusing, but—"

I sat down and took Kai's hand, squeezing it. "Nice to meet you, Simon. You're from London, England? How do you know Kai?"

Flushing, Kai stayed silent, letting me hold his hand.

"We're mates online," Simon said, the initial shock passing, and I noticed he had a nice smile and a cool accent. *Damn it.* I did not want to like the guy or like him for Kai. No way.

"It's, uh, this forum called Geeklandia," Kai said. "We normally talk about Game of Thrones and Doctor Who and geeky stuff like that."

"Right," I said and let Kai's hand go, not wanting to seem like some territorial asshole before we'd even kissed or done anything else. "That sounds fun. Well, Kai, I was going to see if you had any plans, but I see now that your friend is visiting and you probably want to go talk about those geeky things."

Kai opened his mouth, then closed it.

"Yeah, I'm only here for a couple of days, so..." Simon said, laying on the guilt. So, he was one of *those* assholes.

"Oh, okay," Kai said to him, then turned to me, giving me one of his nervous smiles. "Can we do something tomorrow, maybe?"

"Of course, Kai, I'll see you tomorrow," I said, then kissed his cheek, leaving him flushed pink and looking dazed.

Take that, asshole.

***

KAI

Oh my god, what just happened?

I said goodbye to Silas and told Simon I would meet him outside in a minute, then headed behind the counter. Before I could head for the changing rooms, May stepped in front of me, smirking.

"Oh hey, May. Umm, I'm kind of in a hurry."

"Please tell me what I just saw happen actually happened. Please."

"Uh, what?" I still felt flushed because of Silas' cheek kiss, which was pathetic, to be sure. A kiss on the cheek was nothing, yet I felt like he had kissed my lips and smacked my ass or something.

"Please tell me those two hot guys just fought over you like you were the last chocolate chip cookie during rush hour."

I chuckled nervously. "Oh... no."

"Oh my goddess, babe, this is better than any reality TV show I've been watching lately. Seriously, on one hand you have Candidate A, who is the hot daddy type who you've been mooning over for forever, and Candidate B is this hot dorky type who looks at you like you're a hot piece of juicy steak."

I groaned. "No, he doesn't!"

"So, who is he?"

"He's Simon," I muttered, making sure no one is watching or listening. "He's from London. We've been chatting for the past year. You know, about stuff like TV shows and arguing about politics and things like that."

"Wow. Great timing, huh?"

"Stop. It's nothing like that. Simon is my very good friend."

"And Silas? Because, I'm telling you, that thing he did so smoothly back there was definitely laying a claim, babe."

I flushed again. "I have to go," I muttered, then went out back, changing out of my stinky clothes and back into my regular ones, thinking the whole time that there was no way Simon liked me. No way. We were friends. Just friends. And we've never even seen each other before today.

And Silas? Laying a claim? Wow, I hoped so.

Chapter 8

KAI

Conversation with Simon flowed easily, even though he was a bit too touchy feely for my taste. I guess some people are like that, so I chalked it up to personality. I offered to go to a diner somewhere and catch up, but he wanted to see my place, so I took him to my apartment, where I realized that I probably had to offer him the sofa since he'd flown all the way from England and everything.

He had a laugh at my Doctor Who posters and at my computer, always within reaching distance. He even offered to watch some Game of Thrones together.

"Yo, Kai," Jason bellowed.

I was actually relieved it was him because Simon was acting a bit strange. I opened the door to find Jason holding a bong with smoke billowing and spinning inside, like in the movies. Holy fudgecake.

"You wanna join or what?" He waggled his eyebrows.

Normally, I would say 'hell no,' and he would shrug and walk away. But this time, I shrugged and said, "Sure," assuming that Simon would follow. He did, and we all found ourselves on the sofa in the common room, with Jason sitting in the middle, which was hilarious. Like a chaperone.

Not that I needed one. *No, sir.*

Jason handed the bong to Simon, who declined politely and looked at me with big eyes. I laughed at his expression, but also declined.

"So, are you Silas?" Jason asked.

I snorted. "Uh, no, this is Simon, the one I chat with sometimes, from England."

"Oh, yeah, that one."

"How many guys do you know?" Simon asked. "Are you building a harem or something?"

I burst out laughing. "Sure."

Jason guffawed. "I always knew you were interesting enough to keep around, little guy. Now if you could also suck my bong..."

I almost choked on air. "Jason, way to lay on the innuendo." I looked over at Sim. "Okay, I think you're seriously getting the wrong idea."

Simon shrugged. "No big." But he seemed a bit... weird. Like the initial excitement had worn off or something. I was sure this was the case, or maybe he had jet lag. *Yeah, that has to be it.*

"Hey, do you mind if I stay here tonight? I don't feel like going all the way back to the hotel."

Jason snorted, choking on smoke.

"Uh, yeah, sure. You can take the couch," I said helpfully. "I should go and find some sheets or something."

"Or I can sleep in your room."

I froze. "Wait, on the ground? Won't that be super uncomfortable?"

He shrugged.

Jason laughed. "Kai, think about it, man. You are not that slow."

I thought about it and flushed from head to toe. *What the fuck?*

No.

"Hey, you know what? I'll find you those sheets and blankets and pillows. You stay here with Jason, okay, Sim?" I basically ran out of the living room and barricaded myself in my room, except I wasn't so lucky as to have a barricade. As a result, Simon strolled into the room.

"Are you alright, mate?" he asked.

"Yeah," I said, hoping to sound calm and collected and not at all freaked out. "Just looking for the stuff for you to sleep on."

He frowned. "Okay... cheers." Thankfully, he didn't say anything else as I found all the stuff and laid it out on the sofa, making expectant faces at Jason, who finally got the hint and went back into his room, laughing.

Oh, my god.

"Okay, so... shoot, I have to get up early tomorrow," I said. "Do you mind if we turn in for the night?"

Simon sighed. "Sure, Kai, whatever you want."

And that was it. He stayed on the sofa, and I went into my room, telling myself not to lock the door because I wasn't a crazy person. This was my good friend Simon, who, yes, seemed like he liked me, but that didn't mean anything because I liked Silas. So, we could sleep in different rooms without a problem, right? *Right.*

I changed my clothes and ate a Mars bar, realizing it was no dinner and that I was a terrible fudging host. I didn't even know how long he was staying.

Did he say two days?

***

SILAS

Thinking about Kai with that little shit made me see red. I knew I had no claim over the boy and that he could do whatever he wanted. I also knew that even if they did something, it wouldn't be the end of the world.

But my brain didn't want to hear that and spun all night, thinking about Kai being fu—

No.

Maybe if I called him?

I didn't have Kai's phone number, and whose fault was that? So far, we'd always met at Starbucks every day, so there was no need. But just when I needed to make sure that my boy was mine, which he wasn't yet... *Fuck.*

Like always, I called Wes.

"Are you trying to kill me?" he grunted. "I was having the best dream."

"Hey, Wes, can you..." Fucking hell, this was bad. Wes would laugh, and he would have the right to. I was turning into a stalker or a psychopath. "Never mind."

"Hold on. Tell me or I will kill you for waking me up."

I sighed. "Do you have Kai's phone number?"

Silence, then laughter. *Yep, I called it.* "Thanks for your help. I really appreciate your friendship. Bye."

"Wait!" he shouted. "Let me check, for god's sake. I don't have all the numbers in my brain. I'm not fucking R2D2."

I waited for a few moments, struggling to keep images of Kai with his English heartthrob out of my head during the silence.

"There we go!" he said. "Before I give you his number, which, by the way, is creepy as shit... why do you need it again?"

I muttered under my breath.

"What?" he asked.

"Because some asshole from England came to visit him. He was all touchy and looked at me like he was defending his territory. So, I need Kai's number because I need to tell him he can't fuck this Simon guy, all right?"

"You're crazy. You can't do that."

"Why not?" I growled.

"Okay, beast man. First of all, you don't have claim on the boy... yet. Stop growling at me. Second, don't you think that if Kai likes you, there won't be anything happening? He's not some asshole who's going to fuck everyone just because he can. This is Kai we're talking about, the sweet boy who blushes when you pay him a compliment or say something naughty."

I released a breath. "I know... but."

"No buts, okay? Now go back to bed and try to think of something more pleasant than some rando fucking your boy."

I growled again.

He laughed, the fucker. "You're too easy. We have to make this a game. Go to a club and every time a guy looks at Kai and you growl, I take a shot. I'm going to have a monster hangover in the morning."

"Whatever," I muttered. "Thanks for nothing."

"You're welcome."

I tossed and turned for the rest of the night, but I knew Wes was right. It wasn't fair to be acting like a caveman after only one pseudo date. Kai had a choice right now, and I had to let him make it.

If he chose Simon, I'd still have Ellie.

Maybe that would be better for both of us.

***

The next day, I was in such a bad mood that everybody steered clear. To top it all off, Nathaniel Mars kept calling me to meet at his estate. I kept putting it off because I had to go to Kai and make sure we could have that date. The plan was to go there at lunch and ask him out. Just ask him. Like last time. He'd either say yes or no, then I'd know what's what. It was a good plan.

However, when I finally got there, he was sitting at a table with Simon and they were laughing, their knees touching. Great.

I went over to May. "Hey, can I have a cinnamon dolce latte?"

Smirking, she said, "Sure, do you want anything else with that? Muffins? Cookies? A cute smiley boy who's currently occupied?"

She had an innocent smile, but she really was a witch underneath it all.

I scoffed. "No, thanks. To all of the above."

She put her hands on her hips. "So, you're just going to take the coffee and go without saying hello to him?"

"I said hello yesterday," I reminded her. "He looks busy."

"He's not too busy for you, dumbass."

I couldn't hide my frown, and barely suppressed a scoff.

"What, just because you're older than me, I can't call you a dumbass? Kai likes you, but you're being a territorial jerk right now. Go say hi."

I was being told off by a twenty-something-year-old, and I deserved it.

"Fine," I muttered, then took a deep breath and forced a smile.

"Hey, Kai," I said when I reached them.

He looked up with an instant, easy smile. "Hey! Sorry, I didn't see you there. Did May make you your cinnamon dolce latte?"

"You know it," I said, checking out Simon, who was glaring at me. In spite of it, I smiled at him. "Hi, Simon. Are you having fun on your visit?"

"Oh, yes," he said. "Kai has been showing me a great time."

Oh, that little— Breathe, Silas, you can't kill the boy.

I turned to Kai. "Can I talk to you for a moment, Kai? I just have a minute, then I have to go back to work."

"Oh, sure, yeah," he said, then turned to Simon. "I'll be right back."

We went to another table, where I put down my coffee and tried to relax. I looked at him, and the slight flush on his cheeks, his shy smile, the flustered way he played with a napkin, and the way he bit his lip all spoke volumes.

"So, I was wondering," I began, leaning forward to erase the space between us. "Do you want to go somewhere tonight? Just the two of us?"

"Like a... like a date?" Kai asked.

I nodded. "Yes, like a date. I can pick you up at seven from your place."

There was that flush again; I loved it. "Sure... I mean, yes. Definitely. Seven sounds perfect." His smile was brilliant.

"Okay, then." I smiled back and leaned forward to give him a kiss on the cheek, not to lay claim, but because the boy was so freaking adorable that I couldn't help myself. "I'll see you later, Kai."

"See you later," he mumbled.

I felt good about the whole thing. He seemed perceptive and like he wanted to be more than friends, so I would ignore the fact that Simon existed and lavish my boy with all the attention he deserved. That was the new plan.

***

KAI

Holy fudge, Silas just asked me on a date. A real one this time!
I couldn't wait. He seemed annoyed at Simon, who frankly could have been nicer to Silas, but whatever. He was only there for two days, and as much as I liked talking geek stuff with the

guy, that didn't mean I would let anything screw things up with my man.

After my lunch break, it was an insane day, so the only time I stopped working was when my shift was over. May winked at me and wished me a fun date, then I biked to the apartment, where I found Simon and Jason doing yoga together. Or rather, Jason showing Simon how.

I chuckled at the sight of them trying to twist their bodies like pretzels. "Hey, dumb and dumber, what are you guys doing?"

Simon groaned. "I am never doing yoga again, even if it means I'll never have an amazing sex life, as your mate politely pointed out to me."

"Jase, don't be mean to Simon. He has other things to offer a person."

"If you say so," Jason said, smirking.

Simon looked at me funny, while I just smiled at him, being in a supremely good mood because of my upcoming date.

"So, anyway," I said, "I gotta get ready to go out, but will you be okay here, Sim? Hey, Jase, why don't you take him to a bar or club or something?"

"Where are you going?" Simon asked, following me into my room while I picked out clothes. I had a weird feeling that Silas would take me somewhere fancy, in which case I had nothing to wear. *Damn it.*

"What? Oh, yeah. I'm going out with Silas. I don't know what to wear, to be honest, so I'm just gonna wing it."

"Silas, eh?"

"Yeah." I chose a pair of black skinny jeans and a pretty blue button-down shirt, which complemented my eyes.

"How long have you been going out?"

"This would be our second date, I guess. Or first, depending on whether the last time we went out was actually a date or not."

"So, you're not together."

I frowned and looked at him. "I mean, technically, one is only together with someone after some time passes or when both parties decide that is the case, so by that definition, you are correct. We are not together, but we are dating."

He nodded, frowning.

Okay, then... I thought and went back to putting clothes on, even though Sim didn't leave the room like he should have. I felt ridiculous to ask him to leave the room while I changed, since I wasn't some shy teenage girl or something.

"Should I wait up?" he asked. "We can watch an episode of that atrocious show of yours, if you want."

I blinked at him. "Nah, don't wait up. It could be late, and I have work tomorrow. Oh, shoot, and I have to go to the tattoo parlor and apologize to Wes because I've been MIA for the last two nights."

That was great. Just when I had an amazing career opportunity, Simon had to come visit and Silas suddenly decided he wanted a date the next day. This was getting complicated, but I hoped it would get better once Silas and I were together and after Simon left.

If that's what Silas wanted.

Oh my god, what if he just wants to fuck? What if he wants to fuck because he saw someone else was interested, but once we do, he gets bored of my skinny ass?

A mad buzzing broke me from my sudden anxiety attack. It was the intercom. Feeling a bit sick, I went to answer it.

"Hey, Kai," Silas' voice crackled from the old speaker. "Let me up?"

Huh, strange. I buzzed him up.

While Jason waved away his marijuana vapors and Simon sat on the sofa, seeming awkward, I put on my coat and shoes. When I opened the door, a large bouquet of flowers greeted me. Yellow flowers.

Whoa.

"Hey, you," Silas said, handed me the flowers, and kissed my cheek. I flushed all over again. *Jesus, when is my skin going to settle?*

"Hi," I murmured. "Thank you."

Nobody had ever given me flowers. That was both a sad fact of life and a sign that maybe Silas wanted more than just a fuck. *Right?* One doesn't buy a humongous bouquet of flowers for their fuck buddy. Even just thinking that was ridiculous.

"Sunshiny flowers for a ray of sunshine," Silas said with a huge grin.

"Uh, wow," I said, then I put the flowers in a vase quickly, still blinded by their shine and the gesture.

Silas chuckled. "Are you ready to go, Kai?" He wore fancy slacks and a long coat that made him look like a spy. All he needed was a hat. He was so sexy, he didn't even have to try.

"Yep, all ready," I said, then waved bye to the guys and left with Silas, who so far was being a gentleman and a great date.

This night is going to be awesome!

Chapter 9

SILAS

I finally had my boy at arm's reach, which considerably improved my mood. I noticed that he really liked it when I gave him the flowers, when I opened the car door for him, when I offered to help with his jacket, when I pulled his chair, and all those little things that we used to do back in the day when wooing someone.

Courting someone?

Any word I used sounded like I was a character in a historical romance novel, so I tried not to put a label on it. I was just being a gentleman.

Kai deserved the best treatment.

His smile was radiant, he was bouncy and excited and chatty as always, and he looked amazing in those skinny jeans and that tight blue shirt. He looked good enough to eat, which I tried not to think about as we actually ate.

I took him to Bonne Nuit, which Wes went to sometimes. I didn't want to bring him places where Ellie and I had gone, so this was good enough, according to Yelp and my best friend. The people were welcoming, the ambiance was excellent, and the champagne tasted like bottled stars.

All we needed were those talking clocks and cups and thingies from Beauty and the Beast singing about love and curses and second chances.

Maybe compared to our first date, this wasn't as exciting, but I wanted to spend some quality time with Kai and talk to him one on one. So, after ordering for both of us—with Kai's agreement—I clinked his glass in cheers and just watched him, basking in his sunny presence. He licked his lips and looked down at his hands. He was playing with the cloth, which I assumed was a nervous habit.

Always ready to fill the silences, he said, "So get this. I go home tonight, and Jason is teaching Sim to do yoga like some kind of Buddhist pretzel. It was hilarious."

I took a sip and hummed.

"I mean, Jason can do Shashankasana like a pro, but Sim looked like he was going to throw up." He laughed. "I told them to go clubbing or something while we… you know, while we're… here."

I didn't like the fact that he kept mentioning Simon, but I couldn't say anything about it. I also didn't like the fact that my boy was still nervous around me, which wouldn't do, not if we really wanted to try this.

But what if he just wanted sex? Maybe I was scaring him with this dating shit, and if I kept going like this, I would push him away. I hated the mind games of dating. In many ways, I was fine all those years without it. However, I really missed having someone to come home to, so it was a necessary means to an end.

"Kai," I said, "why are you nervous right now?"

He bit his lip and looked up at me, seeming to ponder the question.

"Can I do something to put you at ease? I loved it when we spoke freely on Sunday, and I would like to do the same today."

His body relaxed. "Yeah, me too."

"So, tell me, is there something wrong? Did I do something? Because the whole thing with Simon..." I sighed. "I don't want you to think that I'm some territorial asshole, but it was hard for me to see you with him."

"Really?" he asked, wide-eyed. "You were jealous?"

"Of course I was! I wanted to call you and get you to my place, away from him. I wanted to piss a circle around you, bite your neck, or whatever I could do to make sure he couldn't touch you, but then I called Wes and he talked me out of it, and he was right to stop me. You have your life and your friends; you are free to do as you like, even though sometimes I'm going to be jealous."

He blinked.

Wow, I guess when the dam broke, the words really flooded out. I hadn't intended to say any of that, but now that it was out, I waited for his answer.

"Fuck... I mean fudge," he cursed under his breath and looked at me with those blown-out pupils and flushed cheeks, and I felt my pants suddenly get too tight. He continued in a hushed tone, "I guess I didn't know what you wanted. If you wanted to just fuck, or what, so I was nervous because I like you. I want... well, I want more than sex, you know? Not that I wouldn't... I mean, I would love the sexy stuff too. Obviously." He paused, cleared his throat. "Fudge, I don't even know what I'm saying right now."

I leaned forward, fixing his eyes like a predator eyeing his prey. "Baby, I've wanted you since the first time I saw you, but I want more with you, Kai. More than just your body. But I'm going crazy right now because our food is coming and all I can think about is getting you home in my bed and finally having you all to myself."

His mouth opened, his chest started moving rapidly, and I thought he looked like someone who was on board with anything.

"Should we just go?" he asked, biting his lip.

"Yes," I grunted.

***

KAI

Normally, I wouldn't have begged to leave a romantic date to get in someone's bed, since all I wanted was for someone to romance me, take me on dates, give me presents, and so on. I mean, didn't everyone want that? But the moment Silas laid his cards on the table, and I knew exactly what this was, I just couldn't help it.

Since the first time I saw Silas at the café, I knew what I wanted: him. Now that I knew he wanted me too, I wanted everything at once.

Everything.

We got back in his car and he drove faster than normal, but not breaking any speed limits. While we waited at a stop sign, he reached over to take my hand, kissed my knuckles, and he held it on the middle console between us while he drove with his other hand.

It was so fudging romantic I could have melted.

I hadn't even kissed the guy, and I was all bent out of shape over him.

He had one of those small townhouses, which I found odd for a bachelor, but I didn't ask. The place was very well decorated, albeit a little sparse. I didn't see many personal effects or mementos, just the furniture and appliances. All things he needed, but nothing that displayed his personality.

Maybe they were in other rooms?

"Kai," he said after closing the front door behind us, his voice sounding like a bear coming out of slumber. He hugged me from behind and whispered into my ear, "You have no idea how long I have waited for this. For you. You are so fucking gorgeous and perfect and pure, baby, I almost don't want to spoil you."

"I'm not a virgin or anything," I muttered. "Is that what you think?"

"No, I didn't mean that," he said, still holding me. "I mean that your smiles have healing powers. You're an angel come to earth to heal people with your sunshine, and I'm afraid I might spoil that bright light with my darkness."

My breath hitched as his lips grazed my neck. "Darkness?"

He continued to touch his lips to my neck and landed sweet kisses on my skin, leaving a burning trail behind them, making me crazy. His hands unbuttoned my coat and took it off, then he went back to embracing me from behind. It was so quiet around us, I could hear his ragged breathing and my short, nervous gasps.

God, I hoped he wasn't one of those men who didn't kiss.

He jerked me around and pressed me against a wall with a loud thump. I looked at a different kind of Silas, a hungry one. He fixed my lips with deadly accuracy and dove in for the kill.

He pressed his soft lips against mine, pressed his whole body against mine, and hello, someone was excited. He swiped my lips in a circular motion that made me feel like he was eating them, then he licked and nipped gently, making me open for him, gladly, excitedly, like I was starving for his kiss.

God, could a kiss be any more perfect?

He dove into my mouth, exploring me, tasting me, and touching his tongue to mine. He was dominating me, kissing me so thoroughly I wouldn't have been able to tell you what my name was in that moment. I couldn't say how long the kiss lasted, as I was lost in the moment while he held my head in his hands, controlling how I responded to him. Controlling everything until I felt like I was just along for the ride.

It was perfect.

When he let go of my lips, my skin was tingling like I was in a dream. God, if he could do that with just a kiss…

"Fuck, you taste so good, angel," he grunted in a deep, dark voice that didn't scare me, not even a little. It excited me to the core.

Just because I could, I loped my arms around his neck and gave him a kiss, just like he'd done to me, wanting to taste him thoroughly. He groaned against my mouth, grabbed my ass, and kneaded the cheeks, sending shocks of pleasure throughout my system. As we kissed, I rutted against his big, strong body, against his hardening cock. I climbed him, and he picked me up off the ground as I wrapped my legs around him.

Perfect fit.

We stayed like that for a moment, then he carried me somewhere, but I didn't care where. I just wanted to keep kissing him. When I opened my eyes next, we were in a dark, simple bedroom. Silas laid me down on the bed, watching me like I was his next meal.

He leaned over me and kissed my neck, my clavicle. He slowly removed my shirt, then licked my nipple, sucking on it, making me crazy.

"Ngh!"

"Fuck, I love that sound, baby. Do that again."

"Ngh."

"Yes," he grunted against my skin. "You are perfect. Such a good boy."

"God, please," I whined, running my hands down his arms, over his bulging biceps. "Please, take it all off."

He paused, then took his shirt off and let me see him. He was solid and toned. Not Photoshopped or anything, but he was tight everywhere. Watching his large pecs and his biceps made me salivate. I touched his tight skin and amazing chest, licking my lips like I wanted to bite him.

"Like what you see, little angel?" he drawled in my ear as he ran his large palm down my chest, then my stomach, then over the bulge in my jeans.

"Ngh. Yes..."

He played with my jeans and took them off swiftly, although he grumbled that he hated skinny jeans, making me laugh. He took off his own pants, and we were mostly naked, with only our cocks covered.

Silas covered my body with his. "Fuck, angel, you have to tell me what you want because if you see what's in my mind, you might run away, screaming."

"Please, Silas, I want..."

"What, baby? Tell me."

"I want you to fuck me," I said, and it was the absolute truth. Maybe it was slutty, but I didn't care in that moment. I loved being fucked most of all, and when I was connected with someone like this, it was the best feeling in the world.

He growled, actually *growled*, and pulled me roughly by the hips, then hooked his fingers through the waistband of my boxer briefs and pulled down, revealing my hard, leaking dick. He looked at it ravenously and buried his nose in my pubes, making me moan.

"Ngh!"

"God, you smell so good," he said, then kissed and licked my shaft, up and down, while he caressed my balls with one hand. When I started to writhe under him, he sucked my cock into his mouth.

"Ngh! Fuck." Yeah, so much for not swearing.

He sucked my cock deep into his mouth and his throat. He grabbed my ass with both hands, squeezing, and pulled me even deeper into him, gagging.

Oh my god. Am I fucking dying?

"Ngh. Silas, please, Silas…"

He kept going, and just when I thought I would explode, he pulled back with a loud pop and gave me another ravenous look, this time directed at my face. He slid up my body and kissed my mouth so viciously that it almost hurt, but I loved the pain. I loved everything he was doing to me. It felt like he had bottled some kind of primal need deep inside him and was releasing it.

On me.

When he was done with my lips, he slid down my body again, then raised my legs until my knees were pressed against my chest. "Damn, baby," he said. "Look at that pretty little hole. I can't wait to see it stretch around my dick."

"Ngh! Silas, fuck. Silas?"

"What, baby?"

"Can you, um, this is kind of uncomfortable," I panted, but then I forgot everything because he buried his face between my ass cheeks and made some kind of growling sound that sent vibrations up my spine.

"Oh my god!"

I felt something wet and bulbous touch my hole. I relaxed and opened up for him. He slid his tongue in my hole. I had never felt anything so amazing. Nobody had ever rimmed me.

"God, ngh. Fuck!"

He lapped at my hole and plunged inside, going deeper, then pulling out. He swirled his tongue around, nearly making me explode.

"Silas…" I panted. "Silas, if you don't stop—"

He pulled out of my ass and licked his lips, looking like some kind of wild animal, a demon who wanted my angel hole. *Fuck, that's so hot!*

He kissed my lips again, and said between kisses, "You're so fucking sexy, baby. So tempting. Too tempting for Daddy to resist."

Fuck yes!

"Daddy wants to fuck his little boy. Can he do that, angel?"

"Please, Daddy!"

He growled and gave me a punishing kiss, then stuck his fingers in my mouth. "Get those fingers wet, baby. Get us ready."

I moaned around his fingers as he drove them deeper into my mouth.

He pulled them out and pressed his lips against mine, savagely, while his hand snaked down to my hole and rubbed a wet circle around it. Then, he pressed inside and I was in fucking heaven.

"Ngh, yes! More!" He added another finger, stretching me, filling me with his fat fingers. *Fuck!* "Daddy," I whined. "Please..."

"Do you like Daddy fucking you, baby boy? Do you like your dark daddy finger-fucking your little angel hole?"

"Ngh! Ngh! Yes!"

God, I was flying. I could come just from the dirty talk, but whenever I got close, he slowed down, making me crazy, making me beg.

"Please, Daddy! Please, Daddy!"

He leaned over and whispered, "It's okay, baby boy. Daddy can't help himself; he has to have his little boy."

"Ngh."

He disappeared for a moment. I heard him handling something, probably condoms and some lube, because there was a wet sound. My eyes were closed because I was still flying. When he went away, I whined, "Silas, please..."

"I'm here, angel," he cooed, and I realized he was hovering over me again with that hungry look in his eyes. "Do you want me to fuck you, baby?"

"Please, Daddy, fuck me..."

Grunting, he pressed his cockhead against my entrance and pushed slowly. I could imagine he wanted to thrust hard, but he was taking care not to hurt me. It drove me crazy.

"Silas! Ngh." God, that felt so good. Slowly, he filled me up entirely until I felt his balls pressing against my ass.

"Fuck, baby, that's it. You're mine now."

"Ngh!"

"No one else is gonna touch that pretty little hole," he said as he pulled back out, then thrust back in harder.

"Fuck! Yes."

"Who does this tight little hole belong to, baby?"

"Daddy," I whispered.

He thrust a few times, then changed the angle slightly, and I saw stars behind my eyelids. "Aah! Ngh! Fuck!"

"Yes, baby, that's your Daddy fucking you."

"Ngh, god, please."

He thrust harder and faster, driving with his whole body, his control and speed going for shit as he kept hitting my prostate, making me scream and writhe under him. Skin slapped against skin, the bed shook, and all I wanted was to come. I needed it so badly.

"Baby, I need you to come. Daddy feels too good inside you," Silas grunted, then found my cock and twisted it, and I was done for.

I screamed as I exploded on Silas, shooting cum on his stomach while he milked me dry, my body convulsing.

Seconds later, he groaned and came inside me. He shook and let out another primal growl. "You're my good little boy," he groaned. "Daddy loves to fuck you."

Fuck, I was in heaven.

He gently pulled out and went to get something, then cleaned me up with a wet towel, cleaned himself, and threw out the condom. He then laid down behind me and pulled me against his chest so he could spoon me. We breathed like that, together, raggedly, until we came down and our heartbeats settled.

He kissed my temple.

"So..." I said. "You like the whole daddy thing, huh?"

He chuckled. "Yeah, is that... is that all right?"

"Fuck, yes," I said. "There's nothing sexier than a nice daddy out in the world and a dirty daddy between the sheets."

He laughed, then sighed in contentment, rumbling against my back. Because I was so tired, it must have put me to sleep.

***

SILAS

I had marked the boy, he was mine.

I didn't care about Simon or anyone else just then; all I cared was that Kai was mine and I would keep him that way for as long as I damn could. That he liked the role-playing was perfect. I'd discovered the daddy-boy kink in college with Wes, and although I had not explored it as much as I had wanted to because I met Ellie, I always remained curious. Now that Kai told me he liked it too, I was going to explore the fuck out of it, and him, to my heart's content.

We were lying on the guest bed in the guest bedroom because I hadn't been ready to sleep with anyone in mine and Ellie's bed. If I were honest, I had been thinking about moving because even though I loved some of the memories in this house, I also felt like they were suffocating me. Like I couldn't breathe sometimes from all the memories.

I knew I would not be able to have any sort of meaningful relationship with Kai or anyone else if I clung to the past, so I lay in bed after possibly the most amazing sex I've ever had and thought about moving on.

Ellie would never be truly gone, but Wes was right: I needed to allow happiness into my life. I needed to give my love to somebody. Holding my boy, I promised myself and him that I would do my best not to fuck this up.

Ellie wouldn't have liked that, either.

It was almost like she was in the corner, watching us and smiling, which was strange to imagine. However, I knew she would be happy for me, even though I had denied myself happiness for so long. With a single tear falling down my cheek, I whispered, "Thank you, Ellie," and I let sleep take me.

***

When I woke up, it was light outside, even though the curtains dimmed the worst of the morning light. I realized I didn't know what time it was. I hadn't heard the alarm go off, so I looked around for a phone, a clock, anything.

Kai mumbled something and rolled around, sprawling on top of me, which made me chuckle. He rubbed his nose in my chest. It was too cute.

"Good morning, baby," I whispered, kissing his head.

"Mm, Silas," he muttered.

"Are you ready to greet the day?"

"No," he grumbled, burying his nose against my neck and attempting to go back to sleep.

Yeah, no, I don't think so.

I reached down to his perfect ass and kneaded it. Jesus, it was heaven. That perfect bubble butt would be my death one day. Maybe when I was old and needed Viagra, it would just be too much.

"Ngh," he moaned.

"There's my baby," I cooed and kept kneading as he wriggled and rutted against me, driving me crazy. "Fuck, baby boy, you're going to make Daddy crazy first thing in the morning, aren't you?"

"Ngh," he answered.

Fuck. The little brat knew how to play me already.

Then the phone alarm rang.

"Ugh," Kai grumbled and went back completely under the covers like an incensed little puppy, making me laugh.

"You're not a morning person, are you?"

"Turn it off," he muttered.

Thinking that the stupid alarm had ruined the mood, I got up. "I'll make us breakfast," I said as I climbed out of bed. "And coffee," I muttered as I rubbed the sleep from my eyes.

A few minutes later, Kai was up and entering the kitchen, looking disheveled and cute from sleep. His eyes were puffy and his hair was flying all over the place, but he just sprinted into the room and lunged at me, kissing my mouth and climbing me like a tree.

I grunted, dropping a box of cereal on the floor and lifting my baby up by the ass. I kissed him back with as much passion as I could muster and pressed him into the kitchen island while I squeezed his ass.

It occurred to me that I could have my boy anytime I wanted, anywhere I wanted, any way I wanted, and that was a fucking revelation.

So, I carried him to the sofa and hovered over him while he pulled on my sweats, then I took off his briefs. Completely naked, we kissed and moaned together, and when I found his hard leaking cock, I gave it a few tugs, making my baby groan and arch his back, then I spit on my hand and lubed him up.

I made him lick my hand and lubed my dick as well. Then I took both cocks in my hand—his shorter, leaner dick with my longer, fatter one, a perfect picture of us together—and jacked us off, fast and furious.

"Ngh, Daddy!" he cried out.

I grunted, twisting and tugging while kissing his lips, and then we came together and shuddered against each other. That was the best fucking morning I could remember having.

"Fuck, baby," I panted. "I can do that all day, but unfortunately, we both have to go to work."

"Ugh," he grumbled as we parted so I could finish breakfast—if cereal really counts as making anything—get dressed, then drive Kai to his apartment and go to work, fifteen minutes late for a meeting.

Chapter 10

KAI

I should have taken a shower at Silas', but I just cleaned up real quick so we could hopefully get to work on time, even though as I looked at the clock, I doubted I would make it.

I flew through the front door of my apartment and there, in the kitchen, sat Simon, glaring at me. I could only imagine what I looked like, but whatever. I had to get ready for work.

"Hey Sim," I said as I rushed into my room. I thought I heard him following me, so I said, "I'm running late for work."

"Why didn't you come home last night?"

I yanked on a clean shirt, then looked at him. He was standing there in front of the door with his arms crossed. "Oh, uh, I got held up." Who the fuck asked someone that after a date?

"I waited for you to come back so we could watch something."

What the...? "I told you not to wait up." Where the hell were my other jeans? I pulled everything out of my wardrobe and found them, then threw it back in and changed into my work jeans as quickly as I could.

"Did he shag you?"

I jumped at his tone. It was harsh, his face was pinched in a disgusted mask, and he was flushed and trembling. Suddenly, I felt like something was very wrong. I asked, "Sim, what are you doing?"

"I asked you a bloody question, slut!" he yelled and threw his coffee mug against the wall, shattering it in pieces.

Oh, fuck!

"Sim, calm down. We can talk about this."

"Did you really expect me to come all this way to watch you shag some guy? I thought we had a bloody connection, and now you avoid me like a bloody leper, leaving me alone with your junkie flatmate."

How could I escape? He'd blocked the door. Would screaming wake up anyone? I didn't know. I looked around and located my phone. I would just have to get to it, but first I had to calm him down.

"What the hell, Kai? What kind of a whore are you, walking around, giving your arse to everybody on the second date? I thought you were special, that what we had was bloody special, but you're just like everyone else!"

He advanced toward me with every word, blocking any kind of escape, as I tried to keep calm, slowly retreating away from him, but then my back hit the wardrobe. "Sim, calm down. We can work this out, but I don't like this screaming."

He punched the wardrobe door next to my face, rattling it.

"I don't like you shagging other guys!"

I was panicking. He was shaking in anger and his hands were closing and opening, making fists. Suddenly, he turned around and paced the room, giving me an excellent opportunity to grab for my phone and hide it behind my back. I hoped to God I was dialing someone.

911, May, Jason, Silas... anyone.

"All those hours we spent talking at night. Was it just me jerking off, Kai?"

Gross.

"I found you on Facebook. It was easy. Didn't you want to know who I was? Did you think about me when I thought about you? Did you touch yourself when we were arguing? Because I did."

God, so gross.

My body was betraying me—I was shaking. I wanted to be one of those badasses on TV shows who just kicked the villain's ass, but I was weak and afraid. He was bigger and meaner. He could really hurt me.

God, please, someone.

"Answer me!" he bellowed.

"I'm sorry, Sim, I didn't know. We can fix this."

"How are we gonna fix this, Kai? Are you going to give me your arse now? The one that arsehole pounded already? You're already all used up, you little twat. Who's going to want you now, huh?"

Someone pounded at the door. "Kai! Kai!"

"Jason, help!" I yelled, then Simon covered my mouth and pressed me back into the wardrobe. I could feel his hard cock pressing into my stomach. Was he actually getting aroused by my fear?

Oh, God, please, help me.

"Yeah, that's right, be a good little slut now," Simon whispered into my ear. I tried to wring out of his grasp, but he was stronger. "Even though you're already used up, maybe I can take what's mine anyway and discard you like you did me. Bloody little whore."

The door shook and opened with a lurch. Thank god the locks in the apartment are shit and couldn't hold out. Jason stood there, looking like he was going to fucking kill someone, then lunged at Simon, pulling him off me. Simon's back hit the wall and he grunted, then he hit Jason in the face.

I fiddled with my phone, shaking, trying to call 911, but I could already hear sirens. *Thank fuck*. Simon was about to hit Jason with a metal, miniature TARDIS from atop my dresser. I lunged at him, yelling.

***

SILAS

For the second time in my life, I thought I lost the person I loved. I arrived just seconds after the police and the ambulance, and they were already going up, looking for the source of the commotion.

I followed after them, not giving a fuck if I was in their way or if they arrested me. I needed to find my boy.

Some asshole was trying to stop me when I reached Kai's floor, but I told him I was the one who called them. He said to stay outside until they secured the location, so I did, and it was the longest seconds of my fucking life.

Someone shouted, "Clear!" I heard someone else shouting obscenities, then they dragged a struggling figure outside in cuffs. It was fucking Simon.

When he saw me, he yelled, "You bloody arsehole! You took him from me! Did you like pounding his arse like an animal? Did you like taking him from behind? Did you use him up and discard him, you bloody wanker?"

"Shut the fuck up!" the police officer who had detained him shouted. They dragged him out of sight. If I hadn't been so worried about Kai, I would have tried to break his face in.

"Kai! Baby!" I yelled. "Kai!"

The police officer who stopped me earlier glared at me, probably because I was obstructing his job, but I didn't care.

"Silas!" came the answering call, then a small body rushed out of the apartment and jumped on me like a little tornado. "Silas."

I held him as he shook and sobbed. "It's my fault," he croaked out between gasps. "Jason is hurt."

I wrapped my arms around him, rocking him. Horrified, I realized he was bruised all over.

I'm going to kill that fucker for touching my boy.

They took out someone on a gurney, probably Jason. I looked down at Kai and asked, "Do you want to go to the hospital with him?"

He nodded, sniffing. He seemed to be in shock, because he was still shaking and mumbling that it was his fault.

"Shh," I hushed and squeezed him tighter. "It's not your fault, angel."

I took him down to the ambulance, but they said we had to follow in a car. I led him to my car, put him in the seat, belted him in, and kissed his temple. Then, we were off.

***

They wouldn't update us on Jason's condition because we weren't family.

"This is utterly ridiculous," I muttered, losing my mind and trying to console Kai, who thought that if Jason died, it would be his fault.

I called Wes.

"Heyo."

I talked into the phone while I held Kai and rubbed his back. "Is there a legal way to bribe a health professional?"

"This is the weirdest greeting you've ever used. Why do you want to bribe someone?"

"Because I'm in the fucking hospital with Kai. That fucker Simon attacked him and his roommate, Jason, and we're at the hospital, and they won't tell me anything, and if I get my hands on that little—"

"Whoa, slow down."

I took a deep breath and held it before continuing. "We need to know how Jason is, but we're not family, and Kai doesn't know anyone related to him."

"Right," he said. "And you called me because I have the magic power of compulsion over long distances?"

I rolled my eyes at his ability to joke during an emergency. "I called you because I don't know what to do and Kai is freaking out here."

"Okay, okay, calm down. What about... oh, you're not going to like this."

"What?"

"Nathaniel Mars."

"What?"

"He must have connections, right? His family probably donates to all major establishments, including hospitals, and he probably has a doctor friend who can help you find out more."

I hated the idea, but I was willing to go for broke.

"Okay, thanks, Wes."

He asked which hospital we were in, and I told him. "Good luck," he said before hanging up.

"It's my fault Jason's dying," Kai mumbled, his nose pressed into my neck and his hands pressed against my chest, clutching my shirt. "There was so much blood."

Fuck! I hated this. Hated seeing Kai like this. I had to do something.

I called Nathaniel Mars. He picked up on the third ring and started prattling on about how I finally found my work ethic.

"Nathaniel," I croaked. "Just listen, do you have connections at the Mary Joseph's Central Hospital? A friend of mine was just wheeled in, and they won't tell me what's happening because I don't know any of his blood relatives, so I can't call anyone either. Can you help?"

"Yeah," Nathaniel grunted. "Yeah, uh, hold on." There was some kind of shuffling, then a muffled voice, then he came back on the phone. "I'll call my friend in a minute and get back to you, all right?"

"Thank you," I gasped in relief.

"Of course," he said, then hung up. That was the most human fucking conversation we'd had since we'd known each other.

I kept rubbing Kai down, holding him so he wouldn't fall apart. I suspected he was still in shock, but he wouldn't let the EMTs take him away to assess the damage. He only let them look at his eyes to conclude he didn't have a concussion, which was a relief. Since he moved all right, maybe there was nothing broken, so they finally gave up and let me take care of him.

I couldn't let him go for a second because he screamed bloody murder when I tried. I wanted to bash that fucker's head in for doing this to my boy. I shuddered to think what he'd said, what he'd done.

"It's my fault."

"Shh, baby, it's okay," I said. "I'm here."

We sat like that, in the relative silence of the waiting room, for what must have been a half hour. Then, someone raised their voice out at the reception area. In seconds, a rumpled Nathaniel Mars—which was a rare sight—barged in and frowned at me.

"Hey," I said.

"Hey," he said, looking at Kai. "Isn't that the barista?"

"Yeah. Jason is his roommate."

"All right," Nathaniel said. "Listen, I talked to my friend, and he said he'd meet me here. They don't normally do this, but he said he'd make an exception because of my family's generous donation." He rolled his eyes like he was actually not taking himself so seriously for once.

I liked him better this way.

"Is uh… Is he okay?" Nathaniel asked, looking at Kai.

I barely managed not to growl. "Some asshole attacked him in his apartment, and his roommate got beaten for trying to help."

"Jesus Christ," Nathaniel muttered. He looked up as a tall man in blue scrubs marched toward us. We both stood up, even though Kai was still slumped against me, in my arms. It might have looked weird, but I didn't care. Let them think he was my son or whatever. *Just a traumatized kid, nothing to see here.*

"It's my fault," Kai mumbled, breaking my heart.

The man in scrubs reached us and said, "Mr. Mars, hello, you're here about…?"

"Jason Waxley," I said, recounting what Kai had told me.

"That's right. He came some time ago with a nasty head wound." He looked at Nathaniel. "They stitched him up, though, and other than a concussion, he should be fine. However, with a head wound like this, there's always a chance for amnesia, confusion, that kind of thing."

Oh, thank God.

"Thank you, Stanley," Nathaniel said. "We appreciate your help."

The doctor nodded. "I would appreciate it if you didn't… share this with anyone. It's still against the rules."

"Of course," Nathaniel said, mollifying the doctor.

"Thank you, really," I said to Nathaniel, who looked relieved as well. I focused on my boy next. "Did you hear that, Kai? Jason will be fine."

"Really?" Kai asked, pulling back a little and looking into my eyes. His face was so small and so close to mine. He was all wrinkled and pink and wet and messy, and I just wanted to wrap him up and take care of him.

"Yes, baby, he's going to be just fine, okay?"

He sniffed and hugged me back to his body, finally relaxing, like he had been waiting to know if he'd gotten his friend killed or not.

My poor baby.

Nathaniel sighed, looking away from us.

"Thanks, Nathaniel, really. You're a lifesaver," I said.

He nodded curtly and walked away, saying nothing else. I wondered why he'd done a one-eighty on me, but I couldn't think about that now. All I had to do was make sure Kai was fine.

***

KAI

I was probably acting like a kid, clutching to Silas like I was, but I had never gone through something so jarring. I had never been so scared as when Simon looked at me that way, or when he hit Jason over the head and he fell. It was like something snapped inside me, making me think Jason was dead, and it was my fault.

I kept seeing it over and over in my mind.

Time was mostly frozen. I felt dirty and disgusting, but Wes came to the hospital and helped Silas clean me up and change my clothes. Fortunately, he had the foresight to stop by my apartment and pick up a set from Parker. Silas got really angry when he saw the bruises all over me—on my neck, my arm, and my hips, from when Simon tried to...

I couldn't think about it.

After, I went back into his arms and thanked God that I had someone to protect me from people like Simon. I couldn't believe he had turned on me. How stupid was I that I thought he was a good friend? He was a fudging stranger on the Internet—I should have known better.

Mom always said I was too naïve, always willing to believe the best about people and not seeing the worst. I saw that now.

While Silas and Wes talked, I played with Silas' hair. The only place I felt safe was in his arms. I hoped he didn't think I was annoying or clingy because I clung so tight to him, but I was so scared. I kept running through scenarios where Simon had hit me instead of Jason, where Simon had hurt Silas, where he managed to—

I couldn't think about it.

"Baby, the visiting hours will be over soon. Let's go see if Jason's awake. The nurse said that we can."

I nodded and we went to a bleak hospital room where Jason, the guy who always had a smile and a laugh for me, was lying in a bed hooked up to machines, his eyes closed and a big white bandage on his head.

"Excuse me, has he been awake?" Silas asked the nurse, who shook her head. We sat next to the bed, Silas on a chair and me on his lap. We waited for Jason to wake up, but he didn't. I needed him to see someone friendly when he opened his eyes.

After a while, Silas said, "Come on, angel, we have to go."

"No, I need to be here when he wakes up."

"The doctor said he needs some rest. We'll come first thing in the morning, all right?"

I knew he was right, so I finally agreed.

There was a strange disconnect in my brain between yesterday and today, between the Simon I knew and the one who attacked me, between my amazing night with Silas and the traumatic episode that followed. I was so exhausted that I didn't even realize when we'd reached his house and he carried me inside. He changed me out of my clothes and gave me one of his t-shirts to wear, which was two sizes too large for me. Then, he whispered soothing things in my ear and joined me in bed, holding me tightly, saying he was there for me. Daddy was there.

I fell asleep feeling safe.

Until the nightmare.

***

SILAS

Somewhere around two am, I felt Kai thrashing in the bed. I opened my eyes to find him twisting around like he was trying to escape the covers, as though they were a straitjacket. He was sweating, panting, and mumbling things I couldn't make out. Carefully, I turned the light on and tried to still him.

He twitched, then kicked out, then shot up.

Then he started shaking and said, "It's all my fault."

I held him in my arms while he kept mumbling and shaking and sobbing. I had to remind myself that this was my ray of sunshine. This was the unspoiled boy that I loved, and some asshole had just spoiled him.

The fucker had to go to jail for this.

Chapter 11

KAI

The next morning, we went to see Jason, but he still hadn't opened his eyes, which was worrisome. Silas talked to the doctor, who said it was to be expected, so Silas suggested we go to the police station to give our statements. Even though that's the last thing I wanted to do, I knew he was right.

At the station, a uniformed woman took me away from him, into a small, claustrophobic room, and asked me all kinds of questions.

How did I know my attacker? How long had we communicated on the internet? Had I seen any signs of aggression prior to the attack? She called him a stalker at one point, then asked what he'd said, where he touched me, why Jason was there, and so on. She was like a dog with a bone.

I stumbled a few times and felt supremely stupid, thinking this woman probably thought it was all my fault. I felt hot all over. After she finished with her questions, she asked me to write everything on a piece of paper. It took forever.

She then took me to another room with another woman, who asked me to take off all my clothes, and she then photographed my bruises. I felt humiliated and embarrassed that I was even there, like everyone could see what a loser I was. How I couldn't predict this, how I couldn't fight him, and how it was my fault that I'd been attacked.

When I finally met Silas at the front of the station, he frowned with concern. "Are you okay?"

"Yes," I said. "Can we please get out of here?"

Back in the car, he kept checking on me. "Angel?"

"Yeah?"

"Are you sure you're alright?"

I shrugged.

"I told them everything I knew," he said, "but it wasn't much. I told them what I heard on the call. You did well calling me, baby."

I looked at him. "You're the one I called?"

"Yes, didn't you do it on purpose?"

"I was dialing behind my back, trying not to let him see." Like a teenager with a crush, I had memorized Silas' number, even though it was pointless since calling him would have taken a press of one button. Maybe having a crush was a very good thing.

"You did well, angel. I'm so proud of you."

I shook my head. "Jason's in the hospital because of me. What if he doesn't wake up? What if he's a vegetable now? What if—"

"Kai," Silas stopped me and took my hand. "Please don't torture yourself like this. I promise you, the fault lies in that scumbag who's in jail now, all right?"

"They're not going to let him out, are they?"

He sighed and started the car. "I'll talk to our lawyer and see what he thinks, but the asshole might just get deported since he's not an American citizen."

"Oh, shoot," I muttered. "Wait, we have a lawyer?"

"Of course we do. I have one because I could be sued by unhappy clients. It's just a precaution since they always sign papers that prevent them from suing for damages without cause. I asked him if he knew anything about criminal law. He's not an expert, but he said he would take a look at it."

"Good," I muttered.

We stayed quiet for a while, as I stared out the window mindlessly.

"Kai," Silas said after pulling into the parking lot and turning to look at me. "What can I do, baby? I hate seeing you this way."

I shrugged. "There's nothing you can do. I'm sorry I'm being a kid and that you have to deal with all this fudge. I'm trying to snap out of it, but it's like a mountain of shit piled up on top of me."

He pulled my face toward him and kissed my forehead. "I don't want you to snap out of it, angel. That's not what I meant. You went through something terrifying and I'm so proud of you for being so brave and strong right now. I'm just worried that if you don't talk about what happened with someone who cares about you, you're going to let it fester inside."

"Silas, I... can't."

"But in the future, maybe? You can tell me when you're ready."

I smiled at him. He was so patient. It was a miracle I'd found him. I leaned over and kissed him. "Thank you for protecting me. I promise I'll tell you when I'm ready."

He held me in his strong arms and kissed me back softly.

I was so lucky to have him.

***

Jason opened his eyes later that day, thank God. The nurse called Silas as soon as he did, so we drove back to the hospital.

He groaned, blinking repeatedly. "Holy shit. Do you have my smokes?"

I laughed through tears and tried to hug him, but he groaned again, so I just settled for holding his hand.

"What the fuck did you do to me, skinny man?" he asked in a scratchy voice. He seemed to try to smirk, but it looked like a grimace.

The doctor said there could be some amnesia, and that it was normal, so I asked, "You remember Simon?"

"The dickhead who can't do yoga? Yeah."

"Well, that dickhead got jealous that I slept with Silas, and he… he was yelling and you came into the room to stop him." I looked down at our hands, embarrassed that I had to be saved.

"Good," he grunted. "Never liked him."

"I'm sorry," I mumbled. "You're here because of me. I should have stopped him, but he was too strong and—"

"Hey, skinny man, stop apologizing for shit you didn't do. Now tell me that dickface is in jail."

"He is."

"Good," he said again. "Now, seriously, you have to smuggle my smokes in here or I might die from withdrawal."

I laughed. "I'll see what I can do."

Now that Jason was fine, or well enough, I relaxed somewhat. I even called May, who said that Silas had called her the previous day. I hadn't even realized. She was concerned and told me she could put a spell on that toad Simon and make sure his dick never worked again. I laughed manically at the hospital, making people turn and glare at me. I told her to go ahead and do it.

Then I called Wes and apologized for not being able to come to the shop for the past two days, but he said it was no problem and to take this week off and feel better. He was the best mentor ever.

"Angel."

I turned around to see Silas carrying not one, not two, but *four* puddings. "I stole these from a break room. Don't tell anyone. You and Jason can split them."

I blinked at him and the puddings, then lunged at him and kissed him deeply and thoroughly, thanking him for everything he'd done in the past couple of days. I couldn't believe it was just two days ago that we had mind-blowing sex, and now we were at the hospital and he was so patient and understanding, not pressuring me to do anything, just taking care of me and making sure I ate something.

I really understood what kind of man Silas was that day.

He was my daddy. Not only in bed but everywhere.

***

SILAS

Kai split the rest of the week between going to Jason during the day and spending the evenings and nights with me. He didn't initiate any intimate contact, which I'd expected, so we kept things innocent, just kissing.

I knew we had to talk about things first.

On Friday evening, I came home and called his name, asking if he wanted pasta or lasagna for dinner. He didn't answer, so I swept the house, having a bad feeling. Finally, I found him in my old bedroom.

He was holding the picture of Ellie and me.

"What's this?" he asked. His face was pinched and slightly red. *Damn it.*

"I can explain," I said.

"Is this the girl you told me about? The one you loved? What is her picture doing here? And what's this room? It smells like you."

Fuck.

I felt the room's walls closing in on me. "Angel, please listen to me."

"Are you still seeing her? I mean, how do you even do that? You're here every night. Do you see her during the day?"

"Kai, stop," I snapped. "I'm not seeing anyone other than you."

"Then why is her picture here, and what is this room?"

I took a deep breath, knowing this conversation was long overdue. "Kai, can you please calm down and listen to me?"

His shoulders slumped and he sat on the bed, watching me with anger and distrust in his eyes. I had done this; he was right to be upset.

I sat down next to him and steeled myself. "Her name was Ellie. She was my wife," I said, feeling my throat closing up. "Ellie is dead, Kai. She died."

He gasped. "Oh my god. But why..." he trailed off.

"I'm sorry I didn't tell you, angel." I took his hands. At least he let me. "I wasn't trying to hide it, Kai. I just wasn't ready to talk about it. Do you understand?"

I felt a huge lump rise up my throat, causing me to croak out the words and choke on my own saliva. I closed my eyes, feeling nauseous.

"I'm sorry," he whispered, and as I slumped, he embraced me and patted my back, like I'd done for him at the hospital.

I wasn't ready to share this part of my life. I wasn't ready.

He didn't ask anything and didn't say anything. He just held me and rubbed my back, waiting. I was so damn grateful. I felt the stupid tears prick at my eyes and I couldn't stop them for anything.

We must have stayed there like that for a while because when I looked up, it was dark out and dinner time was long gone.

Like the angel that he was, Kai helped me get undressed, took off his own clothes, and we lay in the bed together. I held him because I needed to feel that he was still there, even though I'd hidden the truth from him.

"I'm sorry," I whispered in the night.

"Shh," the night answered.

***

KAI

Seeing Silas—my strong, amazing Silas—break down like that damn near broke my heart. How did I not know this whole time what he'd carried inside? The whole time I'd known him, he was grieving for his dead wife. I really was completely oblivious to everything happening around me.

But, why didn't he tell me?

I thought back to the first days and weeks I saw him come to the coffeehouse. He was completely closed off, not smiling, just drinking his coffee. When he saw me for the first time, he shook his head like he'd seen a ghost. Then, everything was normal for the rest of that first month, but he came more often. The following few months were more of the same, but he started smiling from time to time. Looking back, he'd looked like he was slowly waking up from deep sleep. The process had taken half a year.

God.

Now it all made sense—the faraway look he got sometimes, not kissing me on our first date, not asking me out even though clearly he was interested, and maybe even the coffee thing he did had something to do with his wife.

His wife. He'd been married.

For how long? What was she like? How did she die? How long ago was it? How long were they married? I had so many questions that I couldn't ask because Silas had broken down at the mere mention of her, so I assumed it was off-limits.

Would he tell me one day? I hoped so.

But for the time being, I had to be patient and tamp down my curiosity for Silas' sake. I felt weird not being able to talk about this huge part of his life, but this wasn't about me. This was about Silas and his healing process.

What did he say to me? That I was an angel come down to earth to heal people with my smiles. God, now it all made sense. My heart hurt for him. I wish there was something I could do, other than wait.

My own hurt seemed like nothing compared to his.

I hoped that we could help each other heal.

***

Silas and I spent that Saturday at home, watching Doctor Who. He'd surprised me by saying that he wanted to check it out and for the first time since the whole Simon thing, I agreed to watch it.

He seemed to love it. "That British fellow is funny," he said. "And he's pretty hot, too."

"Down, boy," I teased. "You're taken."

He kissed my temple, humming. I turned to the side, meeting his lips, and enjoyed a slow, thorough kiss. I moaned in his mouth and positioned myself in his lap, which he took as permission to knead my ass. I chuckled, loving how much he loved to do that. Someone in his pants was getting excited.

Someone in my pants was getting excited, as well.

His phone rang.

"Fuck, let it ring," he said as he kissed my neck, sucking on it. "Ngh."

"Mmm. I love your sounds, baby."

"Maybe it's important," I muttered. What if it was urgent?

He grumbled and let me sit back down on the sofa, giving me an annoyed look. "You're not getting out of this."

I laughed. "Trust me, I don't want to."

His eyes filled with fire as he picked up the phone. "Hello?" He paused, probably listening to whoever was on the line. "What? No, I didn't agree to—" Another pause. "What does that have to do with—" He grew quiet again, but was visibly annoyed. "Yes, I know how much we owe the Mars family." He let out a deep sigh. "Fine, I'll be there."

He hung up, shaking his head. The mood was ruined.

"So, you're going somewhere?"

"There's a charity gala tonight and I couldn't get out of it." He rubbed his hands across his face, then down my arms. We sat on the sofa, staring at the screen where the Doctor's face was paused in a hilarious expression.

"That's okay," I said. "You can't shirk your responsibilities for the Doctor here. Besides, he's not that hot."

Silas laughed and kissed my temple. "You're way hotter than him, baby, which is why I wanted to stay in tonight."

I liked the sound of that.

"However, I have to go. Otherwise, my boss will crucify me." He kissed my neck and pulled back, looking at my bliss-filled face. "Hey, I know. You should come with me."

"What?"

"Yes. It'll be much more tolerable with you there. You can distract me from all the insidious small talk and canapes."

"Uh..."

He kissed my neck. "Please say yes."

"I mean, don't you think... shit ... isn't that going to be full of people you work with, and what if they think I'm..."

"Think you're what?"

"I don't know, a waiter or something?" Or worse, a gigolo. "Anyway, don't I need a fancy suit? I don't have one."

"We'll get you something, baby. Please say yes. It's going to be so much better with you there." Silas looked into my eyes with such hope that I couldn't say no. Plus, it couldn't be that bad. *Could it?*

Chapter 12

KAI

Silas took me to a fancy store with fancy people doting on us while trying to find a suit that was 'perfect for me'. I told him it was no big deal, that we could just rent something, but he looked at me in horror and insisted that he buy me a suit.

So there we were.

A woman handed me suit after suit while I tried things on Pretty Woman style and modeled them for Silas, who seemed very appreciative by the look of his tented pants. *Huh, this turns him on? Interesting.*

"That one," he drawled and came to hug me from behind while I looked into the mirror. "You look stunning, angel."

It was like I was a different person. A person who might not be mistaken for a waiter at this gala thing. The suit was blue corduroy, which matched my eyes nicely, with a champagne-colored silk shirt, but I insisted on no tie. I had my limits.

After that, he insisted he buy me a new coat because mine was old and probably didn't keep me warm, which was such a daddy thing to say, and even though I protested the whole time, he ended up getting his way.

Finally, how could the transformation be complete without shoes?

Ugh.

However, it seemed like it wasn't enough to dress me. Silas also had to bring me to a high-end hair stylist, who looked appalled by my split ends and vestiges of the time I dyed my hair darker.

By the end of my makeover, I probably bore the glare of a mutinous child, but Silas kept mollifying me by giving me praise and kisses.

Soon, it was time to get ready for the gala. Silas put on a beautiful navy suit which matched mine nicely, though he wore a tie because, apparently, he was used to it. Before we left, he almost mauled my face, telling me how hot and amazing I looked and how he couldn't wait to take the suit off me, which was totally unfair, seeing as I then had a hard-on and a stupid gala to go to.

"You're mean," I muttered.

He kissed my nose, and we were off.

A valet greeted us, letting me out of the car and everything. The building looked modern, with two floors with stone steps that led to the first level. There was a red carpet, as though we were celebrities or something. Inside, everything was shiny and sparkly. There were dozens of tables with fancy tablecloths and a sparkling chandelier hanging from the ceiling. The people seemed even fancier—the older men wearing white gloves and the women wearing those shiny night dresses.

Everything and everyone shone.

It seemed like the sole purpose of this event was for everyone to see how fancy everyone else was, which I didn't tell Silas.

He held the small of my back as we entered and looked for our table. Once there, he sighed and waved down a waiter, asking for two champagne flutes, which the guy brought immediately. Everyone was still mostly standing up and chatting—or networking, I suppose would be the case at this kind of event—while Silas and I sat, with him holding my hand and looking at me lovingly.

It was cute.

Before long, an older man with gray in his hair waved Silas down and he took a deep breath. "Come on, time to face the music."

Following him up, I stumbled, but he righted me, smirking. Bastard. I was so out of my comfort zone, it wasn't even funny, and the fancy shoes weren't helping. What do people even talk about at a gala? What was I supposed to say? I was a barista at Starbucks dressed like a Ken doll. I felt like one of those paid escorts who appear at the sides of powerful, rich men. *You're here for Silas,* I reminded myself. *Focus on him.*

So I did, sipping my champagne and following along as any good arm candy should do.

"Darius," Silas said as the old man shook his hand.

"Silas, glad to see you here. Nathaniel was asking for you."

Silas stiffened. "I see."

"The project is going well, I take it?"

Maybe this is his boss?

"Yes, the project is going swimmingly. However, we're not here to talk shop, are we? This is my partner, Kai Moore. Kai, this is my boss, Darius Richards."

Partner? Wow.

The boss man's eyebrows went up comically. "I wasn't aware you had a partner. I suppose now you'll have a reason to come to more of these events?"

Silas didn't say anything.

Mr. Richards shook my hand as I muttered, "It's nice to meet you." The conversation was awkward and stilted after that. Silas soon directed us to some other stuffy people who turned out to be another couple of architects with their wives, one of which was actually nice to me. I kept sipping on my champagne, trying to avoid answering questions, but Silas didn't seem perturbed. He just introduced me to everyone and winked at me from time to time.

It was nice. I knew he didn't actually want to be there, so I figured he didn't take it seriously. I couldn't be with someone who actually wanted to go to these things and brag about their money indirectly. *Wow, what a joke.* However, he seemed to be having fun showing me off, and I couldn't deny that I was enjoying that.

Soon, we were sitting at our table, together with the other architects and their wives. Some event was about to transpire, so everyone was taking their places. "Oh, look," I said with melodramatic emphasis. "My glass is all empty and sad."

"I'll get you another one, baby." Silas looked around, but couldn't seem to find a waiter. "I'll be right back," he said, then left the table.

Great. I was alone, left to fend for myself. I told myself it was no big deal. I could take on those fancy bastards.

"You do know this is a black-tie event, correct?" someone asked next to me. I turned to find the jerkface from Starbucks who'd met Silas there once. I also vaguely remembered seeing him in the hospital, wondering why he'd been there.

"Oh, hi," I said. "Silas said it was okay, so..."

"Do you always do what Silas says?" he asked, examining me with a cold stare. He seemed nonchalant, like he didn't care one way or another, but he also seemed... off, like he had some kind of agenda in asking.

Those days, I felt like I'd lived my whole life with blinders on, but the encounter with Simon tore them away. So, when he asked, I immediately put up my defenses. "Do you always ask strangers personal questions?"

"Only when it is warranted. My friend can be a bit naïve," he murmured, leaning closer so no one could overhear. "He trusts everybody, and I don't like the fact he's chosen to trust a little gold-digger like you."

I felt myself flush at his ridiculous accusation. "I'm not a... I'm not."

"Sure, you aren't. Did he buy you that suit? Those shoes? Let me guess, he bought you that haircut, as well. Is that what you'll be from now on? His kept boy?"

This fucking jerkface.

I fixed him with my death glare as I said, "What about you? Why do you care about Silas and me? Are you jealous you're not in my place or what?"

His eyes flashed. *There. I hit the nail on the head.*

"Don't flatter yourself, princess. You're just a blip in his life. He'll tire of you faster than he'll tire of this event."

My blood was boiling. *Don't kill the guy in a public place, for the love of small animals.*

"Nathaniel," Silas said, rejoining the table.

This Nathaniel person stood up and smiled, shaking Silas' hand and holding on for a bit longer than was polite. "Silas, good to see you. I trust everything with your friend was resolved."

Silas smiled. "Yes, thank you again."

"Anytime," Fuckface said, then looked at me. "It was nice to see you again. Take care." He walked away, looking all smug and shit.

I was furious. How dared he pass judgment on my relationship with Silas!

Was he right though? Would Silas tire of me once he found out that I wasn't fancy enough? Once he was over his grief?

Once he realized I'm just one guy in a sea of many who clamored to be with him?

"Angel, are you okay?" Silas asked, taking my hand under the table and squeezing it.

"What? Oh, yeah," I mumbled.

There was no more time than that because some shortish man with a toupee climbed up behind a small podium amid all the tables and started talking into a microphone. "Welcome, ladies and gentlemen, to the Tenth Annual Charity Gala of the Fine Gentlemen Club."

He droned on...

It seemed the gala was some kind of auction, reinforced by the paddles on our tables next to the appetizers. The money made from it was going to be donated to a children's hospital, where they battled ALS, which was a deadly illness that affected one in five children born in America. Apparently, it affected the nervous system and had a mortality rate of ninety percent.

I was stumped. This was for a good cause, after all, and I'd passed judgment like an idiot. Well done, Kai. Really good work.

Nobody other than the short man talked while the auction was going on, but Silas gently rubbed my hands and gave me soft smiles the whole time. I felt cherished. That jerkface Nathaniel didn't know anything about us. He had to be wrong. Silas would never just throw me away like a piece of ass. He showed me every day how much he cared.

Still... he hadn't shared the most important thing in his life with me. Was it because he didn't see me in his future? Didn't he trust me?

Damn it.

I sipped on the champagne too fast again.

"This next piece is a beautiful interpretation of Jarelli's *Wastelands* by David Sappo. He painted it in 1865 and it survives today. Collectors know this piece to be called *The*

Gem of the Southern Rises. The auction starts at ten thousand dollars."

I choked on my champagne.

Silas rubbed my back. "You all right, Kai?"

I nodded, looking at the uber-expensive painting. It was truly beautiful—a fantastic world with all kinds of creatures populating it, fighting for supremacy. It reminded me of the books I read as a child, of the things that made me love reading and made me fall in love with fantasy and sci-fi, and that made me love world-building and even drawing. The first thing I ever drew was a fictional map.

"Anyone for thirty thousand?"

Silas lifted his paddle.

I stared at him, hissing, "Are you insane?"

He shrugged. "I know you like it. Why not buy it?"

"That's too much money. Don't you dare spend that on me," I said, but he just smirked and kissed my hand, like I'd said nothing.

"Fifty thousand?"

Silas lifted his paddle. I was going to be sick.

"Going once, twice... sold to Mr. Silas Dane from Future and Past Designs. Excellent choice, sir."

"That was an entire college education, just so you know," I hissed at him. "You shouldn't have done that."

He leaned closer and whispered in my ear, "Daddy wants to lavish his baby with gifts, and you are going to let me do that, won't you?"

I flushed. *God, what were we talking about?*

Right, the painting.

He rubbed my hands and kissed my cheek, promising me dirty things with his eyes. Okay, I no longer knew what the argument was about. I spent the rest of the event kind of dazed. Unfortunately, Silas said we couldn't go home yet because there still was a dinner and more hobnobbing that needed done. *Great, more of that.*

Thankfully, he excused us before dessert, and just before we left, he wrote a check and filled some papers to let them know where to deliver the painting.

Then we went off into the night.

***

SILAS

I couldn't help it. When I saw my baby boy stare at that painting with so much wonder in his eyes, I had to get it, even though I would have preferred to get him a car with that money. Still, I couldn't help myself.

He'd given me so much, brought me back to life, and restarted my heart. The least I could do was to buy him a painting.

When we got home, I couldn't wait anymore. As soon as he took off his coat and shoes, I pushed my boy into the wall and started kissing him so viciously it was like I was eating his face. He moaned into my mouth and pressed into my body, making me go hard faster than I thought possible.

He gasped, then pushed me off him.

Fuck.

"Baby, are you okay?" I asked, panting.

"Sorry, I'm sorry," he said. "I don't know what happened. Let's just go back to kissing."

I kissed him softly on the lips and said, "We have to talk about this. Tell me what happened. Did I hurt you?"

"No, of course not," he said, then groaned. He went to sit on the sofa, his face in his hands. "I'm sorry, shit—shoot, it's not you, I just—"

I sat next to him and rubbed his back.

"I don't want to let that asshole ruin what we have," he muttered and looked at me, his eyes full of regret. "Silas, I swear, I'm trying not to, I just—"

"Tell me," I whispered.

He hugged his knees to his chest, making his body even smaller than it usually was. "I talked to that guy for a year, Silas. A year! Not once did I think he was some creep jerking off to my Facebook photo."

"Fuck."

"Yeah... he told me he thought what we had was special and that I ruined it by giving you my ass on the second date. He called me a slut and a whore and he—"

"I'm here," I said.

"He said he should fuck me and discard me like you're probably going to do, then he pressed into me, and he was hard, and I was so afraid..." He trailed off. "Jason came just in time, though."

I held his body, rubbed his back, and kissed his temple. He trembled, sniffing. "Thank you for telling me, angel. I'm so sorry that happened to you, and I wish I could kill him for you without going to jail myself."

He snorted. "Please don't go to jail."

"We don't have to do anything," I whispered. "We can just sit and talk, or we can watch that show you love so much."

"No," he said, looking up at me with those big, beautiful blue eyes. "I can't let him win, Silas. I want you so much, I..."

"What, baby?"

"I just, I want this. Us. You know?"

I pulled him even closer to me, until it was like we were one person. "I know. I want this, too. I like us so much, Kai. Let's try to forget the world for a few minutes and just... be together. Just let me know what you want."

"I want you to kiss me again," he whispered.

I complied. At this point, I would do anything he wanted. I could feel the infatuation growing with every passing day, and even though it scared me, I couldn't stop it even if I tried. This thing with Kai was real and it was special. It was everything I'd wanted and needed. Hopefully, he felt the same way.

I kissed him deeply, thoroughly, letting my tongue explore his mouth. Sweet, delicious moans escaped him and I swallowed them together with his kisses. He tugged on my suit, and I hurried to take it off, together with my shirt, while Kai took off his clothes as well. I pulled off his pants slowly, making sure he wanted me to. His eyes were so dark, so hungry, I realized he needed this, too.

We were mostly naked, making out on the sofa like teenagers. I kissed his neck, sucked on his sensitive earlobe, and kneaded his ass through his boxers.

"Ngh."

"Fuck, baby," I grunted, laying him back down and hovering over my gorgeous, writhing baby boy. "Daddy wants you so much."

"Ngh, please."

"What do you want, baby boy?"

"I want Daddy's cock," he said, shocking my system. He so rarely talked this dirty that it made me a little crazy.

Trying not to take him like an animal and make it good for him, I slowed down and landed sweet kisses on his clavicle, his chest, his nipple, and his stomach. All over his smooth, fair skin. Along those tight stomach muscles honed by hours of biking. Around his navel, and down his happy trail where barely any hair was present. Finally, I tugged at his waistband, looking up at him questioningly.

"Please, Daddy," he panted.

All right, then.

I pulled his boxers off, revealing a hard, leaking cock that demanded my full attention. Just like I had done with the rest of his body, I lavished his cock with kisses and licks and nips, making him undulate under me. When I sucked him into my mouth, he bucked and moaned loudly.

"Aah, fuck!"

I sucked his cock like it was the most delicious milkshake, milking his precum and humming, sending vibrations up his spine, maybe all the way down to his toes.

"Ngh! Daddy!"

I slowed down and pulled back so I could focus on his ass next. I turned him around on his stomach and pulled his ass in the air so I had better access. "Fuck, baby boy, look at that tight angel hole."

I smacked him.

"Ngh! Yes."

"You have no idea what Daddy wants to do to that hole, do you?"

He whimpered.

I bit his ass cheek and smacked him again, making his skin pinken. "Daddy wants to do such dirty things to his little boy. Are you going to let me?"

"Please, Daddy," he panted.

I licked his balls and taint, then I separated his ass cheeks further so I could see his perfect little pink hole waiting for me.

"Daddy's going to stretch that little hole," I grunted, kissing and licking his pucker, then blowing on it.

"Ngh, god, ngh." He arched into the sofa and pressed into my mouth, making me chuckle.

"You just can't wait to be fucked by your daddy."

"Yes, please."

I licked his hole some more, but I didn't have enough patience to rim him. I just wanted to stretch him so I could feel his skin around me. I needed to feel him there, so I spit on my fingers and pushed a finger in, and my boy took it like a champ. I'd noticed how good he was at relaxing his body for his daddy. "You're such a good boy, baby. So good for Daddy."

"Ngh."

I pushed in another finger and kissed his ass, gently nipping at the skin, biting it. Jesus, I could die in that ass. Just get buried in it.

"Daddy," he whispered.

I knew he was ready, so I removed my fingers and looked for a condom. There was one in my discarded pants that I'd brought just in case. I put it on and made sure to use the lube packet I had as well, then lined up against my boy's hole, about to breach his innocence. *Fuck, so hot.*

"Daddy's going to fuck you hard, baby. He can't help himself, okay?"

"Please, Daddy," he whined.

Trusting that it's what he needed too, I pushed into him slowly, feeling that tight heat around my cock and almost coming right then, but slowing down. Taking my boy from behind was doing something to me I couldn't explain. It was such a vulnerable position. He trusted his daddy.

"Such a good boy, taking Daddy's cock."

"Ngh."

I pushed in further and reached the end. I was fully immersed in my boy's ass, not moving.

"Daddy!" he whined, moving his hips, making me crazy.

I smacked his ass once, twice. "Be patient, baby. Daddy's trying to make this good for both of us."

"Ngh, please."

I kissed his spine and pulled back so I could thrust back in, hard.

"Ngh! Yes!"

I did it a couple of more times, grunting with the effort that it took not to fuck into him like some kind of wild beast. I was so close to losing control with him. I changed the angle a little and fucked into him.

"Aah, fuck!"

There we go. I did it again, making him moan and undulate under me.

This was going to be over pretty soon, so with that in mind, I pushed his legs back into his chest and fucked him in a fetal position, thrusting hard and fast.

"Daddy! Oh god! Ngh!"

"Daddy's not going to last, baby. You're too good," I grunted and repositioned him so he lay on his stomach while I pressed my body on his and invaded his hole from behind. This angle allowed me to fuck him so deep it felt like I was fucking his insides.

"Ngh! Oh god! Daddy!"

"Yeah, baby," I groaned. "Fuck, baby. You have to come. You have to come for Daddy. Make all the cum Daddy wants."

"Ngh! Daddy!"

I fucked him hard and fast and deep, feeling him convulse under me as he moaned his release, shaking and leaking, I assume somewhere on the sofa, while I fucked through his climax, like a madman, and finally, *finally*, I came inside my boy, grunting like a man possessed.

"Fuck!" I cursed, relaxing on my boy, staying there, connected to him. "Jesus, baby, are you okay?"

Kai laughed. "I'm fine, though I think you fucked my brains out."

"Oh baby, fuck, you make me go crazy. I don't even know what I'm doing when you're under me like that."

"Mm," he hummed. "I like making you crazy."

"I know, you little brat."

He snorted.

I finally pulled out of him and threw away the condom, then pulled him into my chest and chose to forget about the fact that we were basically lying in cum. Whatever, I didn't care.

I kissed his hair. "You're amazing."

"No, you are."

"No, you are," I said, smirking.

"No, you are."

"We can go like this forever, you know," I said, pressing my nose in his hair, smelling vanilla and sweat. "Hey, I was thinking about something."

"All the ways you can fuck me?"

I burst out laughing. "I'm not a complete caveman, you know. I was actually thinking about asking you if you wanted to reduce your hours at Starbucks."

"What? Why?"

"Because I want you to be less tired. I want to make sure you have energy for your apprenticeship, and because I selfishly want to spend more time with you."

"Mm," he hummed. "I don't know."

"Think about it?" I asked.

He sighed. "Okay, I will. But I refuse to be your kept boy and let you pay for everything, you hear me? I will pay for dates and anything else that we're sharing. That's my condition."

"You're being ridiculous. I'm perfectly fine paying for all our expenses. I want to, Kai. As the daddy I have the right to, don't I?"

"I'm not just your boy. I'm also a full-grown man."

"If you weren't, what we just did would have been highly disturbing."

He snorted. "Just... we'll both think about it, yeah?"

"Fine," I said. Before we went to sleep, I forced myself to get up and clean us up. While I grumbled about it, Kai laughed and said that's what Daddies are for, then the little brat fell asleep.

Jesus, I loved the boy.

Chapter 13

KAI

On Sunday, Silas and I—or rather, Daddy and I—fucked every which way, pretty much the whole day. From morning blow jobs to fucking on the couch to fooling around when he made lunch to him taking me on the living room floor when he couldn't take my teasing anymore, we went at it all day long. With the exception of a call from Wes, who was told by an annoyed Silas that he was busy burying himself into the tightest ass in the universe before being hung up on, we weren't interrupted. It continued while we tried to watch Doctor Who and failed, then well into the night.

I was well-fucked, thank you very much.

Finally.

On the next day, I was back at work, hugging May, whom I'd actually missed. "Hello, you hag. Did you miss me?"

She waved me off. "Are you kidding? I was so lonely here with my sad little voodoo cups and coffee, but I made up for it by making everyone my slave and having a sex orgy in the back."

I snorted. "Wow. Okay."

She winked at me, cackling. "And you? I'd ask if you were lonely, but you have this whole sex glow that's actually a bit out of control."

I felt hot around the ears. "Shut up."

"No, really, if anyone comes too close, you'll probably zap them full of sex radiation. You better be careful with that weapon of mass destruction."

I rolled my eyes as I stacked up the empty cups, getting them ready for later use, next to the coffee machine. "Seriously, can we not talk about sex right now, seeing as we have to focus on work? I'd hate to spend the day with a tent in my pants, and how will your poor little heart take it?"

"I'm fine with it. My girl has a strap-on dildo, and she regularly pegs me, so the sight won't give me a heart attack or anything."

I stared at her. "Are you serious?"

She shrugged.

Oh, my god.

We spent the next hour serving the early risers, then the work crowd, and I thought about what Silas suggested from time to time. If I truly wanted to give my mentorship a chance, I needed to make a decision.

When lunch came around, I looked up and there, in all his beautiful and sexy glory, was my boyfriend. Partner. I smiled at Silas.

"Eww, seriously?" May asked. "You're going to give each other moony eyes? Why do I always have to be around for this and suffer?"

"Shut up," I said, still smiling. "I can't be bothered with your complaints right now, since I don't even care about anyone else other than my sexy god of a boyfriend."

"Holy goddess, you're whipped."

I chuckled. "Don't I know it."

"Hi, angel," Silas murmured when he finally reached us. May was on the register, and I was leaning next to the muffin stand, facing him.

"Hey, you," I said, licking my lips. I couldn't help it. I was thinking about all the naughty things we'd done the day before, and judging by the way his eyes suddenly went dark, I was certain he did too.

"You both are contagious right now. We should pull up a CDC tent around here," May muttered, then asked what Silas wanted.

He frowned and looked at the menu. "Uh, well..."

That was weird. I looked up at the menu and asked, "Caffe Americano, maybe?"

He rubbed his chin. "You know what? Make me a macchiato."

"O-okay," I said, confused at the turn of his daily ritual. It had been there since we'd met, and now, suddenly, he was changing it. *Why?*

I made him the macchiato, throwing him suspicious glances, but he was just smiling and waiting for it. When I handed it to him, he gave me a quick peck on the lips and winked at May, who was glaring and saying something about germs around the food and drinks. I rolled my eyes and stuck my tongue out at her.

Silas sat at a table nearby and drank his coffee while he looked at his phone.

"Why don't you take your break?" May suggested.

However, before I could join Silas, the jerkface from the gala appeared in the door and headed for my boyfriend's table. *Great.*

He sat down with a smug demeanor, as if everything belonged to him, and said something to Silas. Damn the stupid distance and being unable to eavesdrop.

"Why is that jerk back here?" May asked, but capped it as the asshole came over to the register and ordered an English tea, explaining exactly how to make it in painful detail. He watched me like a hawk and made a couple of suggestions, making me bristle, but I kept my mouth shut. He was a customer.

He left an outrageously large tip like before and went back to Silas.

"No offense to your boyfriend, but he could choose his friends better," May said, putting the tip in the jar like it was a wriggling slug.

"He's not his friend, he's a client," I muttered, throwing an eye on their conversation. The jerk kept showing Silas something on his iPad and touching his arm, which really pissed me off since he knew we were together and I was in viewing distance. He was doing it on purpose. *Ugh!*

"Do you want me to bespell his dick and balls to fall off?"

I snorted. "Actually, that's not a bad idea."

***

SILAS

For the love of god. Changing the entire garden's layout. Really?

I was at the end of my rope with Nathaniel Mars. He might have helped Kai, for which I would be indebted to him for a while, but that didn't mean I could let him play with me like I was some kind of pawn or a chew toy.

I took a deep breath. "Nathaniel, listen, Joe and I have already laid out the costs, and he has ordered the materials, so—"

"So what? I can pay for all that."

Fuck. Me. And him. And everyone. Mostly him. "I think it's a mistake to make changes at this stage of the project."

"No offense, Silas, but this is my estate, my project, and my garden, so if you can't make it work, then maybe..." He shrugged.

"What?"

"Maybe I should hire someone else."

I was about to say that we could work it out, but the relief I felt at his words was so palpable, it hit me in the face. I smiled. "If you think that's necessary, far be it from me to argue with you. Do what you feel is best."

Nathaniel gaped at me. Gaped. "Well, I... I mean, that's not necessary. I suppose we can go with your old designs for now."

Wow, that actually worked. "Great, that's perfect. Now excuse me, I have to go back to work." I got up, but he touched my hand, stopping me.

"You'll come by tomorrow to see the hedges? I tried to talk to Joe, but he's being obstinate about it."

Don't kill the man, don't kill him. "All right, Nathaniel," I said, struggling to keep my voice calm. "I'll come see the hedges." Then, I walked away, but not heading for the door, because I had to stop by the register and kiss my baby on the cheek.

He looked happy, which sufficiently improved my mood.

I turned toward the exit and offered Nathaniel a curt nod. He frowned past me, and I followed his gaze to find him glaring at my Kai. I didn't like it. If he ever did something to make Kai less than happy, if this even was what it looked like, I was going to be the one firing him.

There was no way I was ever letting my angel go.

***

KAI

Holy shit, I had missed the smell of marijuana hitting me in the face when I came home from work. Jason had returned from the hospital, so I went to see if he needed anything.

"Hey, Jase, you okay in here?" I said through the vapors, coughing. Oh my god, I was practically getting high just standing there.

"Oh, hello, my sweet little roommate. Look at what I made with my mouth. Those over there are circles, those are flying pigs, and that there is an amoeba."

Wow, he is really high. "That's impressive mouth-smoke art, my friend. Listen, I gotta go to JustInk. Are you going to be okay in here?"

Jason still wore a bandage, but he said he could change it himself and that he was fine, flying in the clouds as he was.

"Okay, then," I said, then went into my room.

I hadn't been there in a few days because I'd been staying with Silas. He didn't even ask me why; he just accepted it as something I needed, which was perfect. I still wasn't ready to be back there, but I had to face it. I looked at the dented TARDIS and the blood, which of course no one bothered to clean. *Why would they?* I stepped around the mess to the wardrobe, which Simon almost broke trying to get into my pants—

Stop it.

Shaking the memories away, I hurried to change my clothes and spritz on some aftershave, hoping the weed vapors wouldn't carry into my new workplace. Without another look at the room, I got out of there like a bat out of hell.

I biked to the tattoo parlor, arriving with five minutes to spare, and found Jazz talking to Matthew in the foyer. As soon as she saw me, she came and gave me a bear hug. Her breasts were as big as watermelons, so being hugged by her was an interesting experience. Squishy.

"My sweet Kai, are you okay? I heard what happened."

"Mfine," I mumbled, and she let me go. "I'm okay, really."

"If you say so. What are you going to do for us today? Oh, I know, you can practice on Matthew. He doesn't mind being a pincushion."

Matthew flipped her off.

Wes peeked out his head and hollered, "I need my apprentice! Man, I love being able to say that. It's like I'm Don Corleone or some shit."

I laughed and hurried to join him in the back after telling the others I'd see them later. Wes, at least, did not treat me like I was broken. He immediately told me to take my place and keep practicing. I sat down and turned my attention to those poor banana peels. In a way, tattooing them was nice, therapeutic. It made me forget I was someone who was stupid enough to get attacked in his own apartment. Everyone kept saying it wasn't my fault, and I know they meant well, but they didn't understand how many signs I'd missed. One night, I laid awake in Silas' bed remembering every conversation, and I could see how I'd misconstrued and plainly ignored so many obvious red flags.

My mom would have—

Shit! I won't have to tell my mother, will I? I was on the family health insurance plan. Maybe she wouldn't notice?

Thinking about this made me slip and catch my thumb in the tattoo gun. Wes cursed and helped me clean up the blood.

"I'm sorry," I said. "I'm so sorry, it just slipped."

"Brother, do you know how many times I did this to myself?" He shrugged. "Don't even worry about it. Go home, though. It's getting late, we can continue tomorrow."

I thanked him. He really was the best boss slash mentor. It didn't hurt that he was Silas' friend, as well.

Before I left, I remembered something. "Wes?"

"Mm?" He had already returned to working on something at his station. His back was turned to me.

"Did you know Ellie?"

He froze and stopped fiddling, then turned. I thought he would be angry or distant or defensive, but he just seemed very sad. "I knew her. She was... lovely." He sat down and smiled. "She was the light of day, you know? The person who gives more than they take, who gives life to everything around them. She was curious about everything, adventurous... Brilliant, really." He let out a deep sigh. "It was a tragedy when she died. The world lost one of the best fucking people, you know?"

"How did she die?"

He cocked his head. "Silas hasn't told you, has he? Look, Kai, you have to be patient with him. He took it hard, you know? He was a ghost for three years. He just looked alive, but he wasn't, not really."

I swallowed the painful lump in my throat.

"Just let him tell you when he's ready. Don't push it, okay?"

I nodded. "Sorry, and thanks."

"Anytime, kid," he teased.

I flipped him off and left to the soundtrack of him laughing behind me. It was nice to have more people to count on. Silas' friends were starting to feel like my friends, which really made me feel like we were real.

I wouldn't screw it up. I would wait.

Chapter 14

SILAS

The bliss of fucking Kai in the morning was quickly replaced by a polite reminder that I was to go to Nathaniel's Estate and look at those damn hedges.

For fuck's sake.

The guys were there, Joe and his workers, among which Pete and Garber, whom I knew because they'd helped me with another project a few years back. Who knows, maybe they'd helped me again recently, but I couldn't remember much from the dark post-Ellie period. When I greeted them, they looked at me in a strange way, which was fair enough.

"Hey, boss," Joe said.

"Nathaniel's actually your boss, you know."

Joe shrugged, adjusting his hard hat. "I would rather have you as my boss, so I guess I'll just call you boss until my wish is fulfilled."

I laughed. "So, what are we doing with the hedges?"

He groaned and explained that there was no way to make them as high as Nathaniel wanted because they would obstruct visibility and some of the trees would have to be cut down. The shorter hedges helped the matter.

"What does he want, anyway? A weird maze where he sacrifices virgins and releases werewolves after them?"

I snorted. "It wouldn't surprise me."

Nathaniel joined us in about five minutes. "Good morning," he muttered. "Beautiful day for a ride."

"Pardon?" I asked.

"Do you ride? Horses," he clarified, smirking.

"Yes, I know what horses are, and... I haven't in a while."

Ellie and I used to ride. She loved it, but since she'd gone, I stayed away from some reminders.

"How about a ride, then?" he asked, a jock stick already in hand. "Come on, follow me to the stables."

Before I could protest, he was leading me to stables where the most beautiful horses I'd ever seen lived. There was a pure white one, who appeared to be a sweetheart, a wild black one, like a demon who kept kicking his confinement, and a few brown ones, hoofing when they saw their master.

"I don't think I have time—"

"Nonsense," he said as he handed me a saddle. I knew how to do it, so I sighed and saddled the horse he led over to me, the white one.

"Her name is Sadie. She'll go easy on you."

"I'm not a complete beginner, you know," I muttered as I watched him saddle up one of the brown horses.

"What about the black stallion?" I asked.

He shook his head. "We'll have to sell him or put him down. He's too wild."

I felt sick at the thought of people putting down this magnificent creature because it couldn't be tamed.

"If you can't find a buyer, you might find a rescue for him."

"You're such a do-gooder," he said, laughing as we led the horses out of the stables and into the garden.

The moment I got up on the horse and took off, I felt invigorated. I imagined Ellie would love this.

I laughed into the wind. I was flying.

When we finally got back to the mansion, I was beaming, like my face had split in two and light was coming out of it. I wished Kai were there, and I thought of calling him to tell him about the ride, but before I could do that, Nathaniel dragged me out of my moment.

"My grandmother is in the dining room," he said, "waiting for us to join her for tea."

I blinked. "Your grandmother?"

"She's a worldly creature. She's traveled all the corners of the world, and I'm lucky to have her to myself for a whole day."

It was strange to see Nathaniel so... relaxed. Human. It reminded me of the Nathaniel who was at the hospital. Because this version of him was more palatable, I agreed, and we went into the big house to find a frail little white-haired woman. Her chin was up as she squinted at me.

"Nathaniel, my boy," she said, greeting her grandson. "Who have you brought me?"

Nathaniel laughed. "This is my... friend, Silas. And this is my grandmother, Gertrude Mars."

I wondered why he didn't say we worked together, but didn't pay it much heed. I kissed her shriveled hand and said, "Pleasure to meet you."

"He already has better manners than you, boy," Gertrude said, then focused on me, looking me over like I was a prized horse she was considering for purchase. "You seem to be young and healthy. I approve."

"Uh, thanks?" I said, confused. What did she have to approve of me for?

"Please, sit," Nathaniel said, indicating a chair next to him. He tried to pull it out for me, at which point I came out of my stupor and picked another chair.

Gertrude snorted. It was very unladylike.

The maid brought us tea and we had a relaxed conversation about Paris, where Gertrude had just returned from. Since I'd been there and seen the Louvre—with Ellie—I could hold my own in the conversation.

It was a strange day, to be sure. So many things reminded me of Ellie and I had so many questions for Nathaniel, but I relaxed, intending to leave thinking for a later date, when I wasn't so flustered and perhaps after I called Kai to tell him we had to go horse-back riding this weekend.

I wanted him to experience the freedom, if he hadn't already.

Nathaniel walked me out after the tea. "The old hag likes you, and she doesn't like anyone."

"Well, good. Now, I've told Joe about the hedges, but he won't budge. I need you to approve of the height before he—"

Nathaniel waved me off. "Fine, whatever you two have decided on."

Fucking hell! I spent all this time trying to appease him, and he just gives up? Trying not to explode in his face, I took a deep breath and said, "All right, then, I'll see you." Before I could leave the house, he took my hand and pulled me back.

I stumbled.

He was not stronger than me, but he had the element of surprise. Looking at my lips and licking his, he pulled me closer to him.

Fuck! I punched him.

"Jesus Christ!" he hollered. "What the hell?"

I punched a man who's worth billions in his own millions-of-dollars estate. As I realized the ridiculousness of the situation, I couldn't help but laugh.

He glared at me. "Really?"

"Sorry," I panted. "I'm sorry, I just—" I couldn't stop laughing. I'd wanted to punch Nathaniel since we'd started working together, and now that I had, I felt better.

"As long as you're enjoying this," he said, holding his head up and his nose closed to stop the bleeding.

I pulled myself together. "Sorry, I apologize. You just caught me off guard. And by the way, what was that? Were you trying to...?"

"Kiss you? Yes, of course."

My jaw fell. "What? Jesus, why?"

He laughed ruefully. "Because I like you, for heaven's sake! Haven't I shown you already? I've been trying to spend time with you, calling you, but you wouldn't pick up, and now that we finally had our first date—"

"Whoa." I lifted my hands. "That was *not* a date."

"Yes, it was," he said.

"No, it wasn't. For a date to happen, the two people involved should know it's a date, and since I didn't know it was, then it wasn't."

He looked exasperated. "Fine, will you go on a date with me? Just put me out of my misery? I'm running out of ways to—" He stopped talking.

"I can't go on a date with you because I have a boyfriend. You know this."

"The boy toy from Starbucks? Come on, isn't his expiration date nearing? Just give me a ballpark time span. I'll wait."

Jesus, that man was delusional. "Look, Nathaniel," I said carefully. "I'm flattered, really, but... Kai is my partner. I love him. He's the only man I go on dates with."

Nathaniel deflated. "You love that... barista?"

"His choice of profession has nothing to do with my feelings for him. And, not that it's any of your business, but he's a very talented artist."

"He's trying to use you for your money. Surely you must see that."

"The only thing I see, Nathaniel, is that you've been trying to manipulate our professional relationship for months for your own personal benefit. I think I'm right in saying that we should both take some time, reconsider our priorities, and maybe sever this agreement, for both our sakes."

"You would throw away a million-dollar contract for that boy?"

"I would throw away everything for him," I said, trying to make him understand. "He's not a rebound for me. He's the real thing."

Nathaniel shook his head, but he stopped talking. I think he finally understood it wasn't going to happen. I almost felt sorry for him.

"I'll see you around, yeah?" I said, but didn't wait for an answer before I left.

We would have to talk about the project at a later date, I supposed, but I couldn't feel bad for screwing it up. Even if I was fired, I could not work with someone like Nathaniel Mars. If Kai was working with someone who constantly tried to get in his pants, I would not have liked that at all.

So, I wouldn't do that to him.

Chapter 15

KAI

I finally did it—I asked Stew if I could get reduced hours, and he shrugged and said it was fine. Looking at my new schedule, filled with relief.

"I'm going to miss you," May said. "Remember me when you're getting married on a cruise surrounded by your new rich friends."

I snorted. "Don't worry, I'm going to ask you to be my best man, and if I know you well enough, you'll probably show up wrapped in shawls and offer tarot readings for obscene amounts of money."

"Aww, you *do* know me well!"

I couldn't wait to tell Silas that I'd done what he asked, and to be perfectly honest, it wasn't because he asked. It was because he was right—I needed to give JustInk more of my attention. It could become my future.

But when Silas came by the coffee shop at lunch, I knew something was different. He came with a small bouquet of flowers, which he gave to me with a bashful smile, and he kissed my cheek, making May pretend-gag. Then he treated me to anything I wanted and kept stealing little touches and kisses, making even me a little nauseous, but mostly confused and dazed.

What was happening?

"Is everything okay?" I asked.

"We'll talk about it tonight. You're going to JustInk after this, right?"

"Yes..."

"Can I pick you up at, say... eight o'clock?"

"Okay..."

"Great," he said, grinning and giving me another quick peck on the lips. "I'll see you then, baby." Then he smiled at me as he backed out of the shop and tripped over someone, apologizing profusely.

He waved, I waved back.

When I went back to May, she was trying not to laugh.

"Wow, that guy is whipped," she finally said and burst into what I could only qualify as a manic witchy cackle. She even snorted.

"What the what?" I muttered. "That just happened, right?"

"Mm-hmm."

"Why was he acting so weird?"

"Because he's madly in love with you and he wants to spend the rest of his days with your skinny ass?"

I flushed. "We haven't—no, it's not—"

"Oh, you haven't dropped the L-bomb yet, have you? Well, from what I saw today, he's about to, so you better be prepared, babe."

Oh my god. Love.

Did I love Silas? Well, of course I did.

Wait, what?

Yes, I loved Silas. I was in love with him, which meant that if he told me he loved me, it would be a good thing. Right?

Oh my god.

I didn't expect this. I mean, I had hoped that we were heading that way... one day... in a hazy semi-near future. But wasn't it too early?

Fuck.

My head was all messed up for the rest of the day, but I had to go through throngs of people, a hundred orders, and then a few banana peels before I even got to see Silas again.

When I finally did, I was exhausted.

***

SILAS

How did one tell their significant other they loved them?

With Ellie, it had just come out after sex one time and it stuck. I was planning a nice evening with Kai and a sexy night, and maybe after that we could...

Fuck, I didn't know.

I didn't want to be the creep who rarely said the words to anyone, or who called his best friend to ask if he should propose marriage after he said them.

This was crazy.

I waited with little patience for the day to pass so I could hurry home and make my special roast chicken with harissa and schmaltz recipe, to make everything perfect and ready for our romantic dinner—I even bought candles—and then pick up Kai.

He was curiously quiet on the way home, but I guessed he was exhausted since he'd worked more than ten hours. He wasn't shaking his leg like usual. He was so still I had to make sure he was awake, and when I peeked at him, he was peeking at me, smiling shyly. *Weird*.

"Hey," I said.

"Hey back," he said.

It was cute.

We sneaked peeks at each other and smiled like love-sick teenagers, which really bode well for my plans.

When we finally got home, I helped him out of his coat.

"It smells... weird."

I laughed. "Good, I hope?"

"Yeah, what is that?"

I led him to the dining table, set with utensils and the fancy plates I kept for special occasions, and lit red candles.

Kai watched me bring the food, then asked, "Why are you acting strange?"

"I can't have a romantic dinner with my partner?"

"Of course you can," he said, sitting down and looking at the dish, which I was now piling onto his plate. "Mm, smells delicious. Family recipe, is it?"

I nodded.

He took a bite and closed his eyes. "Oh my god... this is so good! I want to have its babies. Do you mind, baby?"

"Uh-huh. Just remember, only I can make you that dish properly."

He laughed, piling up food in his mouth and wolfing it down in ten seconds flat.

"Jesus, some romantic dinner, you're already done," I teased. "Should we have some light conversation, or should we just go to separate beds and avoid each other like we've been married for fifty years?"

"Talking's fine. Like... you can tell me why you were so weird today."

"When?"

He chewed his lip. "At lunch."

"What? I wasn't weird at lunch, baby."

He sighed. "Don't lie to me."

Well, shit. He was right, wasn't he? I was weird, and I was lying. What a great way to build trust between partners. "I'm sorry, Kai. I think I'm messing this up. Maybe we should start over. I've just been nervous—"

"Why have you been nervous?"

This was the time to tell him I loved him and I wanted to spend the rest of my life with him. Unfortunately, something in my brain broke, making me say, "I went out on a date today. Accidentally."

"What?" Kai shouted, wide-eyed. "With who?"

Fucking hell, what did I just say? "Uh... Nathaniel Mars?"

Kai closed his eyes and sighed. Then he glared at me. "You were on a date with that... that... jerkface? Are you serious?"

"It was accidental, baby. It wasn't actually a date. I don't know why I said that. Nathaniel thought it was a date, but I didn't know."

"How does one go on a date accidentally? Or without knowing? Did you fall on him? Did he kidnap you?"

I snorted, then coughed. Laughing now would be so bad. "Okay, look, I went out to see Nathaniel's hedges—fuck, I mean his garden's hedges, okay? He was driving me and Joe crazy about their height. Anyway, I went, and he asked me to go horse-back riding with him."

Kai crossed his arms. "Horse-back riding? You rode horses?"

"Yes?" Shit, this sounded bad. "Then he introduced me to his grandmother—" *Holy wow, this sounded worse.* "And then he tried to kiss me."

Kai was vibrating. His skin was flushing.

"Baby," I said softly. "It wasn't a date, okay? I didn't know it was. I was just caught up in wondering why in the world Nathaniel Mars was doing those things when we were basically arch nemeses."

Kai sighed. "Because he likes you. I could have told you that."

"I know that now, all right? I didn't know before. And when he told me, I set him straight. I reminded him I had you and I—I only date you, angel."

Kai pursed his lips.

"Is it really that bad? I didn't know how he felt and I did not kiss him. Actually, I punched him. He's probably going to fire me any day now and—"

"You did what?" he said, his mouth agape. "You can't lose that project. You said you'd be able to buy a new place after this."

Did I really tell him that? Christ, I hadn't even realized. "It doesn't matter. My priority is that I never find myself on a date with Nathaniel Mars ever again."

Kai snorted. "Good."

I reached out my hands. "Are we okay, baby?"

"Yes..." He sighed, letting me hold his hands. "I'm not mad, obviously. You didn't know what was happening, and you can be quite oblivious to people's advances."

I smiled and kissed his hand. "You're the best." I kissed it again. "You should have seen his face when I told him I loved you. It was priceless."

"What did you just say?"

Fuck.

***

KAI

Okay, I could not sit anymore. I had to stand up and walk around the room because otherwise I would explode all over the table. "You said—you told—" I was furious, flapping my arms around like a seagull.

"Baby..."

"You told Nathaniel Mars before you told me?" I shouted.

Silas winced.

That was loud. I probably woke everyone up in a five-mile radius. It might have even reached the jerkface's ears.

"I said it to make him see he couldn't... you know, have me."

Silas came closer to me, but I pushed his chest. "The most romantic moment of my life, and you told my arch-nemesis—mine, not yours—before you told me. What the fuck is wrong with you? Now when people ask about it, I'm going to have to say you had a very romantic moment with Nathaniel fudging Mars, and not me!"

"Angel, calm down, please. I'm sorry."

"You're crazy! You go on accidental dates, you blurt that you love me to somebody else, you give people huge flowers and expensive paintings, and you—you—"

I deflated, letting my arms fall.

"Can we do this again, baby?" he said, slowly advancing toward me like I was a skittish animal. Then, he grabbed my hips, paused to check, and satisfied, he drew me closer and hugged me. "Not that I don't love arguing with you, but can we maybe rewind and try this again? Or I should say, can I try this again? I went about it backwards. I'm sorry."

He could really mellow me down, the bastard, so I hugged him back.

"Fine," I muttered.

He kissed my temple, my forehead, my eyes, my nose, my cheek, and my lips, staying there a while, then pulled back and gave me the sweetest smile, filled with so much affection and care. "I love you, angel."

I gave up. "I love you, too."

His whole face lit up like those stupid candles of his. He kissed me, picked me up in the air, and spun me, making me dizzy.

"Put me down!" I bellowed, laughing.

"God, baby, I'm so happy. We should celebrate," he said. "Oh, I know, you should move in with me."

"What?" I gaped at him. Was he crazy?

"What? Is that so unusual? I want you to live with me. Then you can be here every morning and every night."

"I'm here most mornings and nights."

"But not *all* of them. I want you here with me," he said, kissing my lips. "Will you please think about it?"

It was all happening too fast. Normally, I would freak out, but for some reason, I wasn't. I waited for the claustrophobic feeling to grip me, to make me feel trapped or something, but it never came. I just looked at Silas as he looked at me, and it felt... right. Like it was meant to happen this way.

"Okay, I'll think about it."

He kissed my nose. "Great, now I can relax and maybe finish my dinner, because I'm starving," he said, like nothing out of the ordinary had happened. He sat down to eat and kept smiling. *Holy shit.* My world had just turned upside down and he was just eating.

After dinner, he got this wild look in his eye, picked me up over his shoulder, and smacked my ass a couple of times. "Daddy needs to punish you for yelling earlier," he said, then he fucked me in the hallway because we couldn't make it to the bedroom.

What can I say? I felt a bit wild myself.

Chapter 16

KAI

The next morning, I told Silas about my reduced hours at Starbucks, and he kissed the hell out of me, happy as a clam.

"This means we'll have more time for dates and trips," he said, beaming.

"And," I reminded him, "I can go to JustInk more often."

Silas waved that off as an afterthought, but I could tell he was just teasing. He knew how much the mentorship meant to me. He was a good daddy, helping me out with my life, not just turning me on in bed.

Many people would shudder at the thought of someone trying to control their life, but it's not like that. He gave me direction, without which I would flail and stagnate. I always needed someone to point out the way. I might be stubborn at first, but eventually I would come around and it would work out.

It's just that I didn't always know what to do next, but Silas seemed to help bring things into focus. Without pushing too much.

When we settled into the new schedule of fewer work hours and getting home earlier from JustInk, Silas started taking me out on dates more. We went to an art gallery, the cinema, and even to a fantasy convention where Silas was stupefied at some of the costumes people wore. I was Doctor Who, of course, and he was himself because that was good enough anywhere.

We went on trips on some weekends. He took me to a cabin in the woods for a romantic getaway and to the next city over to see the aquarium. Overall, I was having the best time of my life with him.

Finally, a couple of weeks after we talked about it, I raised the question. "Hey, remember when you asked me to move in?"

Silas stopped chewing his food and blinked at me. "Yes?"

"Do you still want to?"

"Angel," he said, squinting at me. "Of course I want you to. Is this a hypothetical question or are you finally saying yes after making me wait forever?"

I rolled my eyes. "You're such a drama queen. It's been two weeks and I haven't even been back to my apartment once."

"Which means you're wasting your money on something you're not—"

I raised my hand. "Yes, okay, let's move in together."

Grinning like an idiot, my boyfriend cursed, got up from the table, and picked me up over his shoulder, then smacked me on the ass and said, "That's for making Daddy wait so long."

What followed was too wild to put into words.

That weekend, I moved in with him, which was the first time I ever lived with a partner. I hoped I wouldn't have to move back out, ever, because I really believed Silas was it for me. He was the one.

***

I was stepping out of JustInk, waiting for Silas to pick me up, when my phone rang. Without looking at the caller ID, I picked it up.

"So, you appear to have moved," my mother scolded.

Oh, shit. "Mom! I, uh—"

"Kai Lovebug Moore, did you move out without telling me? I sincerely hope you're still in the city because otherwise I have nowhere to sleep!"

I winced at the full name, mostly because it's the worst hippy name in the history of names. "Sleep? You're visiting?"

"Yes, you said I could, remember? And now I'm looking at your former roommate making strange positions with his body, smelling like a sixties hippy camp—by the way, I'm not complaining—but little Johnny has started sneezing—"

"Oh my god, Mom! You brought Johnny? Are you crazy? What if I lived in a building full of drug lords and pedophiles?"

"You forgot to mention, dear." She laughed, actually laughed. "Now, will you tell me where to go next, or is this some kind of cruel scavenger hunt to torture your mother with? Don't forget, I carried you in me for some time longer than was necessary and you stubbornly resisted getting born for ten hours, so for those two reasons, you owe me at least a little bit of courtesy."

I sighed. "Mom, I'm sorry."

"It's all right, dear. Now, tell me the new address, and I'll be there in a jiffy. The cab driver left, but I'm sure I'll find another one who sings out loud to Cher songs in a delightful Pakistani accent."

At that moment, Silas pulled up, and I said, "I'll come get you, mom. Stay there."

"On a bicycle? Will it fit us?"

161

"You're hilarious. Just stay with Jason for a few minutes and I'll come relieve Johnny of his newfound allergies, although I doubt that's the first time he's smelled weed, knowing who my mother is."

"Ten hours, honey, ten hours. They didn't give me drugs, either, so imagine having kidney stones for that amount of time, but a bit to the south."

"Great image, mom. I'll see you in a bit."

I hung up and shuddered.

Silas smiled as I got into the car, and I took a deep breath. "My mother is in town to visit and she's brought the baby and now they're with Jason standing in a cloud of weed smoke and I owe her for the ten-hour labor—"

"Whoa, baby, slow down. Your mother's with Jason right now?"

I bit my lip. "Do you think we can—"

"We can pick her up," he said, then pulled away from the tattoo parlor and headed toward my old building. "You don't have to be so nervous. I'm actually excited to meet her."

"Did I mention she brought the baby and that they're staying over and that my middle name is Lovebug?"

Silas burst out laughing. "*Lovebug*? Jesus, do you think maybe you could have told me when I wasn't driving so I might not risk both of our lives in a fiery car wreck?"

"Sorry," I muttered. "So, we're picking her up and giving her shelter, right? I still kind of like her, despite the awful middle name and the constant guilt trips about being a stubborn birth."

"Stop worrying," he said, still laughing. "I would love to meet and shelter any woman who gave birth to you."

"Even if she was a junkie or a hooker?"

"Even if she was a serial killer."

"Whoa," I said, smiling. "You must really like me, huh?"

He winked. "Of course I do."

When we pulled up, my mother was already on the steps in front of the building with her baby and her suitcases, like a homeless woman.

Silas and I got out of the car. While he quickly introduced himself and put her luggage in the car, I kissed her and Johnny, then proceeded to glare. "Could you have given me notice? Or stayed inside where it's warm?"

"It's been a while since I've smelled the stuff. I quit, remember? I was afraid you'd have to pull me out on a gurney. Johnny really needs his mother at this fragile young age."

"You can't overdose on weed, mom," I said as I helped put Johnny in the backseat. "Don't be overdramatic."

"You can, the way we Moores do it."

We all got in the car and Silas drove off.

"So, it's Silas, is it? And who, pray tell, is Silas? And why doesn't a mother know anything about her son's life?"

"Uh—"

"You didn't tell your mom about me?" Silas asked, looking hurt.

"Guys, can we just relax for a minute?" I asked. "I'm sorry I didn't tell you, mom, but every time I tell you about a guy I'm seeing you start asking about grandchildren. Maybe that has something to do with it. And Silas, I was going to tell her when we got a dog or an actual grandchild, you know."

He snorted.

"Oh, how great to hear," my mother deadpanned. "So, how far away are the grandchildren? Or have you just started banging?"

"Mom! Johnny's right there."

"Oh, he knows quite a variety of naughty words. I taught him well."

Silas laughed, the traitor. That's the last thing I needed, my mother and boyfriend in cahoots with each other. God help me.

When we got home, she looked at the house with an approving nod. We got her luggage and the baby and went inside. Once there, I said, "So... here we are. Home, I mean. I...uh... live with Silas at the moment."

"Did your room flood?" she asked.

"No."

"So you live here because—"

I rolled my eyes. "Silas asked me to move in with him and I said yes?"

"Aha! I knew the grandkids would come soon. My psychic said just last month that I should expect positive changes in your life, and that is why I came."

"You came on a word of a psychic," I drolled. "Of course, you did."

Meanwhile, Silas was making dinner, which also impressed my mother. She mouthed something obscenely complimentary about him, which I ignored because she was my mother, not my gay best friend.

I helped her put Johnny down for a nap in the master bedroom. She assured me that once he was out, he was out.

"So, Silas," she said as we went back into the living area. "What do you do?"

"He's an architect," I answered.

She shot me a look. "Can't architects talk for themselves?"

Silas laughed and said, "I'm a chief architect at Future and Past Designs, ma'am. I have worked there for twelve years."

"Please, call me Stella. Also, that's quite a run. You like it there?"

"Yes. I get to pick my own projects, and I've always loved my job."

"That's excellent! See what happens when you find your path, dear? I've been telling Kai to look for more art opportunities, but he's stubborn. Maybe once I'm gone, he'll see how wise I was when I was younger."

I snorted into my glass of wine.

"Has Kai told you about his JustInk apprenticeship?" Silas asked as he flipped something in a pan. "He's studying under one of the best tattoo artists in the city."

"No, he forgot to mention that. It seems he's decided not to tell me anything."

"Mom! I don't tell you things because then you call every day to see how it went, then you complain when I ask for some space."

"You didn't need space when you were in my womb. I don't understand why it should be any different now."

Silas snorted, then covered it with a cough.

I'm surrounded by traitors.

As always, Silas' cooking was excellent. Even my mom liked it and asked for the recipe. She told Silas a bunch of embarrassing childhood stories, which he seemed to file away for later teasing.

An hour later, my mom was exhausted from traveling and asked about turning in for the night. I couldn't be happier.

***

SILAS

Kai looked flustered as he started looking for sheets and blankets for his mother.

"Baby, it's okay. She's not staying forever, is she?"

"I wouldn't be surprised," he deadpanned. "I'm sorry I put them in the master bedroom. If you want, I can put her on the couch."

"Don't you dare. The master bedroom is fine. It's now our guestroom, anyway."

"Okay..." He relaxed.

"Darling son?" Stella cooed from the hallway. I opened the door to see her serene, smiling face. She was a young-looking fifty-year-old woman with a little bit of gray in her hair and twinkling eyes. They were blue like her son's, and she appeared to have his smile and his humor. I loved it.

"Could I trouble you for sound-canceling headphones? I did not get the warning that I'd be listening to my son rutting in the stables."

"Mom!" Kai flushed. "Nobody's having sex here, okay?"

"Oh dear," she said, looking at me. "I'm sorry, Silas, my boy is usually very sexually active. I don't know what's gotten into him."

I chuckled. "Don't worry, Stella, we'll spare you any unbecoming noise for the duration of your stay. It's not a problem."

"Why didn't you ask for two sets of headphones?" Kai asked. "For Johnny, too."

"Oh, Johnny doesn't know what his bottom is for, so really, he doesn't know anything about sex or reproduction. Why would he need headphones?"

"Oh my god," Kai muttered. "Always a pleasure talking to you. Excuse me while I go bleach my ears and change my surname."

"It was nice meeting you, Stella," I said. "I'll see you in the morning."

Kai slammed the door in her face.

I raised an eyebrow and met Kai's eyes with an unspoken question.

"I was afraid you'd say something even more welcoming, and I really don't need her to get any ideas. This is a nightmare."

"Baby, it's okay," I said, hugging him from behind. "Your mother's a character, to be sure, but she's kind of like you. And I love you, so I like her."

"I am not like her!"

I gave him an unamused stare.

"Okay, maybe a little, but please don't throw that in my face after the day I've just had. You should know better by now."

"I apologize," I husked, nipping at his earlobe.

He pulled away as though he were stung and hissed, "No kissing or anything else! We are not fucking right next to my mother!"

I laughed at his horrified expression. "All right, baby, calm down. Breathe."

"I'll breathe when she's gone," he groaned, then we started getting ready for bed. Kai ended up putting a pillow fort between us 'just in case', and even though it was a good idea in theory, in practice he ended up sprawled on top of me.

***

"Good morning," Stella said, looking at me from the kitchen island. She appeared to be making something for the baby.

I returned the greeting, then froze. The picture of me and Ellie was next to Johnny. Kai came in after me and gave me a curious look, then turned to his mother.

"Shit—I mean shoot—mom!" he said, then hurried to hide the photo. "Don't touch people's personal things."

"I simply wanted to know who this beautiful creature was. She has the eyes of an old soul and the smile of an empath with a good heart."

"Mom, stop," Kai hissed. "It's none of your business, okay?"

"It's all right, angel," I said as I went to join them. Kai looked so apologetic and flustered, but I realized that I no longer felt flooded by grief when I looked at that picture. At some point, it turned to warmth and good memories. "Her name was Ellie. She was my wife. She died three years ago, but I still carry her in my heart. I just forgot to put away the photo because I haven't been sleeping in that room. And, thank you, she did have a very good heart."

Stella's face softened. "I'm so sorry for your hurt, Silas. I would have been more sensitive had I known."

"Don't apologize. It actually reminded me that it's time to put some things to rest. When I met Kai, I was so entrenched in my grief. I could hardly see anything else, but his smiles kept me grounded. They healed me."

I kissed his head.

"That's so lovely. You two are very well matched."

"Mom," Kai hissed.

"Thank you," I said to Stella, ignoring his protests. Then, I turned to him. "I should have told you about Ellie much sooner, Kai, and don't think I haven't appreciated your patience." Then, to his mother again, "Your son is a saint, Stella."

"Guys, stop," Kai mumbled, rolling his eyes. He turned to me. "There's no rush. You can tell me, or not tell me, whenever."

"I know, angel." I kissed his lips briefly, full of love for the best person, well one of the two best people I had ever known. "Now," I added. "Let's get ready for work and figure out our evening plans. We should take your mom to Venoro's."

"Uh, she might not have a fancy dress in her bags."

"I always have a fancy dress with me," Stella said, "in case some rich architect decides to take me out to dinner."

She laughed, I laughed, and Kai rolled his eyes and looked like he was going to die from embarrassment.

Chapter 17

KAI

My boyfriend was a saint. He was not only nice to my mother, but he pulled all the stops, making sure her stay was great. She only stayed three days, during which we all had dinner together, including the baby—we found him a little baby suit with a fun bowtie.

It was the longest we'd gone without sex since we started. The moment she was gone, we picked it back up.

The days went on as usual, bleeding into one another. I only worked at Starbucks three days and trained the rest of the time at JustInk. I occasionally met May and Jason for beers and shots and had a hangover in the morning.

Life was good.

It continued until the middle of November, when Silas became more withdrawn than usual. Quieter. I asked him if work was hard, but his big project with Nathaniel Mars was actually going well, without the jerkface hounding him about anything. There was no other stressor that I could see.

I mentioned this to Wes.

"The anniversary of Ellie's death is coming up," he said. "I was afraid this would happen. You know, Silas can be very stubborn and stoic. Sometimes it's best to snap him out of it. Just talk to him."

"What if he's not ready?"

"He has to be. To move on fully, he needs to be able to let go of the past. Or, rather, he needs to break free from its hold over him, you know?"

I nodded, thinking about it the whole time while Silas drove us home. He didn't speak, just smiled wanly. When we got home, he started cooking. We ate, then watched an episode of Doctor Who, cuddling on the sofa, but he wasn't there mentally or emotionally.

I was afraid that if I pushed him, he would get defensive or lash out. I didn't want to hurt him more than he was already hurting.

But what if I needed to do it? What if he needed me to get him out of this state? I was his partner. If not me, then who?

"Silas," I said, "can we talk?"

He didn't answer.

"Baby?"

He was already sleeping. He'd looked exhausted, like he hadn't been able to sleep, and I wondered why I didn't wake up when he did. Maybe he was trying to be quiet.

I wanted him to trust me. I wanted him to finally open up to me.

Why couldn't he just do it?

***

The next morning, Silas basically ignored me. There were no sweet kisses, no touches, no teasing—nothing. It was like Silas had reverted to himself of nine months ago. When I talked to him, he barely listened or looked at me.

I imagined he was remembering his life with Ellie. Or worse, he was remembering her untimely demise—every detail about it.

If that's what he was doing, I didn't want him to suffer.

I was considering how to breach the subject when the doorbell rang. I wondered who it could be so early on a Saturday. We'd gotten up because we were used to getting up early, even though it was usually a day of rest for us.

I went to open the door.

On the other side were a woman and a man, in their sixties maybe, looking at me with puzzled expressions. They both had dark hair and dark eyes. The man had a familiar nose and the woman had familiar eyes. It was like together they formed a puzzle picture that I'd seen before, but I couldn't put my finger on it.

"Hello, is Silas here?"

"Yes, he's just in the shower. Who are—"

"Savannah, James," Silas said from behind me. He had put on sweats and a t-shirt in a hurry. "I apologize. I overslept."

I frowned. *Who are these people and why are they here?* The woman was holding some kind of dish, and the man was holding her.

They looked supremely sad.

Oh, god.

"This is Kai," Silas said. "Kai, these are Ellie's parents."

They murmured greetings and came into the house, heading for the kitchen, where the woman put the dish on the counter and stared down at it like it held some kind of universal secret.

"Kai, could you give us some time?" Silas asked.

Stumped, I looked at him. "Are you sure? I can—"

"Kai, please," he said, his tone making it clear he would consider no further dissent.

I didn't know what else to do, so I left, heading for the bedroom. I resisted the urge to eavesdrop because this was too intimate of a moment. I owed Silas at least that measure of respect.

Why did he ask me to leave, though? I understand this is about Ellie, but I live here now, don't I? My stomach hurt.

Being patient felt impossible.

***

SILAS

I looked at Ellie's parents and fell back into the old pattern. Savannah opened the dish, which was Ellie's favorite, and James set the table while I gathered Ellie's things—small mementos and pictures that we'd collected in a box that I'd put in a closet. I placed them on the table like a shrine and we ate in silence.

As the meal wrapped up, we each shared something we remembered about Ellie.

Savannah remembered how Ellie used to want to do things, then get in trouble for it. Like that one time she wanted to learn how to skate and broke her hip.

James remembered how Ellie liked to buy postcards from every place she went to and collect them on her wall over her bed.

I remembered how Ellie and I used to try different dishes from different restaurants. She was never afraid of trying anything, even if it looked or sounded questionable.

It was a familiar, comfortable ritual, even though something was niggling at my brain. When the time came to leave for the park, I paused and wondered if I should tell Kai. He shouldn't have to worry where I was.

I knocked on the bedroom door.

Kai appeared, frowning. "Hey."

"Hey, we're going out for a bit. I'll be back later, all right?"

"Oh, okay."

"I'll see you later," I murmured, then left him, rejoining the parents of my dead wife.

That day marked the day she died four years prior.

***

There was a spot near the edge of the park where she used to run, and where she ultimately died in a freak accident. A car swerved onto the pavement and skidded sideways into a lamp post, then slid over the grass onto the runner's path, right into Ellie. The driver had been going over the speed limit, and was drunk.

That was in the morning.

Half an hour later, I got the call and went to the hospital, but she was already gone.

Now Savannah, James, and I went to the spot to leave flowers and think of her. My own parents hadn't been interested in me after I'd proclaimed I was bisexual, so when I finally moved out, they'd been relieved. They barely knew Ellie—barely even knew me—so my family was these two people by my side.

"So, Silas, how have you been?" Savannah asked.

"Good. Working, like always."

"And who was the young man in your house?"

I winced. I didn't even know how to tell them I'd moved on. Would they hate me? "I, uh, he's... you know—fuck, I'm sorry." I leaned forward, holding my head, preparing myself for whatever came next.

"For what, dear?"

"Kai is my partner. I met him a few months ago. We've lived together for a few weeks now, and I—" I paused, steeling myself. "I love him."

173

Savannah nodded. James just watched something in the distance.

"I am glad you have found happiness again," Savannah said. "Our Ellie would have wanted it for you."

I shook my head, sitting up. "I'm sorry. I didn't mean for it to happen. I wanted to stay with Ellie forever, I really did."

"You will stay with Ellie. She is in your heart, as she is in ours. But that doesn't mean you should hold yourself back from living your life. You can love more than one person, Silas. You are allowed to be happy."

I sobbed at her kindness. "Thank you."

She held my hand and squeezed it. "Oh, son, we are so lucky to have you in our lives. If it's all right, we would like to meet Kai, also."

I couldn't believe it. "I would love to introduce him to you. Maybe next month?"

"Sounds good," James said. Despite his stoic demeanor, he was always more emotional than even Savannah. He spoke rarely, to hide the tears.

We sat there in loving silence and I thanked God for not only giving me Ellie and another set of parents, but also for giving me Kai.

Chapter 18

KAI

He went out.

He went out with the parents of his dead wife, and it was like I was a stranger to him. Silas was probably ashamed that I was in his house when they came. That's why he only introduced me as Kai, not his partner or boyfriend.

It was time to face the truth—I was a rebound.

He didn't trust me. Didn't trust me with the most intimate part of his life, and I couldn't stand it any longer. I had waited for as long as I could, but the way he dismissed me this morning was the last straw.

I was no one, not even worthy of acknowledgment, just a passing ship in his life, so of course he wouldn't want her parents to know me. He wouldn't even let me help him.

Feeling clobbered, I collected my things in a bag. I couldn't go to JustInk because Wes was Silas' friend. Silas knew where I lived before, so I couldn't go there, either. If he wanted to talk—which I did not want to do, not then nor ever—he could find me. So, there really was only one place to go.

I called May.

After we hung up, I left the house, took a cab, and started to cry.

***

SILAS

I couldn't wait to go home to Kai and talk to him. The conversation was long overdue, and I felt foolish and cowardly for postponing it for so long. Perhaps I was afraid of the emotions that would come out of me. Or I was afraid of his reaction. Or I was simply afraid of remembering.

Whatever the reason, I couldn't be afraid anymore. Kai was my partner, whom I loved. It was time.

Back at home, I called out for Kai and went to look for him in our room, but he was nowhere to be found. At first, I thought maybe he was in the bathroom, but he wasn't there either, nor was he in the backyard. He was nowhere.

Something niggled at my brain.

I went back into the bathroom. His toothbrush and other products were missing. With a heavy heart, I went into our bedroom and found some of his clothes were gone, as well, along with his laptop.

Fuck.

No.

I felt numb. He couldn't have left, could he? He said he loved me. He moved in with me. He—

He did everything right, and I basically acted like he was a stranger this morning.

Fuck!

I dialed Kai's phone, but it went straight to voicemail. It did the same thing three times in a row, which either meant he was very fast at rejecting my calls, or he'd turned his phone off.

Next, I called Wes, who answered after a few tries.

"You know," he said, sounding irritated, "I actually have a job I need to do from time to time."

"Is Kai there?"

"No, why?"

"He's not here. He's taken his stuff and—fuck." I didn't feel like myself. Without Kai, I would have nothing again. Without his smiles, I only had the pain. Without loving him, I would be a dead man again.

"Fuck," I kept cursing. "It's my fault."

"Calm down. Yes, it probably is. Hey, I'm sorry, mate, I know what day it is today. Did you have an argument or something?"

"Ellie's parents came. I just—"

"You shut him out and acted like he wasn't even there."

Oh, how well Wes knew me.

"Yes," I croaked. "I'll try Jason next."

"Just don't let him get away, okay? He's a good one."

"I fucking know that!" I hollered, realizing immediately I was out of line. "I'm sorry, this isn't your fault, Wes."

"It's fine. Now, go," Wes said, then hung up.

I was an imbecile who let the only good thing that had happened in his miserable life walk out of his house.

I drove like a madman over to Jason's. When I rang the bell, he answered in his speedos. *Jesus.* The whole place was smoked to full capacity and he had a dazed expression, like he wasn't even really there.

"Hey, man, you come to ride the magic dragon?"

"Uh, no... is Kai here?"

"Nah, man, he hasn't been around, but I'll tell him you looked for him. Maybe he's at the tattoo place. Or maybe aliens abducted him. Shit, they could really hurt the poor skinny dude." He looked serious about the last one, so I made a mental note to check on him later.

"Tell him to call me if you see him, okay?"

"Right on, man." He closed the door in my face.

Okay, what now...?

May.

I headed to Starbucks, praying to God that she was working today. I didn't have her phone or address. It was stupid of me not to have that information, but now wasn't the time to beat myself up about it.

I basically flew inside, finding May at the register. *Thank fucking god.*

"May, have you seen—"

"Don't even try. I am not letting you anywhere near Kai right now."

"May, please," I said, ready to grovel. A customer approached the counter, so I let him through and waited there like an idiot.

"May," I pleaded again, to her back, as she made the customer's drink. "Please, listen, I made a mistake. I need to apologize to him."

"How convenient to say that now," she retorted as she handed the drink to the man, who left muttering about coffee house drama.

"I fucked up, all right? I should have talked to him sooner. I know that, but in my defense—"

She quirked an eyebrow.

"I have no defense, I know. I just want him back. Please, May."

"And how do I know you won't hurt him again?"

"I love him, May. More than I have ever loved—" I closed my eyes, sighing. "I just need to talk to him. I need him to know that he's the best thing that's ever happened to me. The only thing I need in my life to be happy. I need to know if he still loves me."

"Maybe you should wait a few days."

I was close to tears. "Please, May, I can't wait for this. I need him to know now."

"For goddess's sake, you two are the worst. It's always drama, drama, drama. First there were the other men, now this. Honestly!" She blew out a breath. "Fine, I'll give you the address, but if you hurt him again, I will put a spell on you that will not allow you to sleep through one night without wetting yourself."

"Wow. Okay."

"Good." She wrote down her address and gave it to me. "And it should go without saying—no make-up sex at my place."

"You got it."

***

KAI

May's girlfriend Leslie was home when I got to May's place—she'd given me her key and everything—and when she saw me all choked up and puffy, she proceeded to show me her dildo collection.

Well.

It was a very impressive collection, to be sure, and I suppose her strategy worked because I didn't cry or think about Silas while she explained the difference between each brand, detailing the pros and cons, like one of those review sites that have tables of all the features of every brand of computer.

The doorbell rang.

"Oh, it's probably that sweet flyer dropper guy. Last time it was for pregnancy vitamins, and I told him we didn't need any, but he didn't believe me, seeing as we both have working wombs and everything."

I snorted.

She opened the door. "Hello? Who are you?"

"Hi, I'm Silas, looking for Kai?"

"Oh, he's not here, actually," she blurted out, but the effect was diluted by the fact that when Silas peeked in, I was clearly visible.

Shit.

"Kai, can I talk to you? Please?"

"I don't want to," I said. "Go away."

Silas, still at the door, stoppered by a tiny but mighty lesbian, said, "I'm not going anywhere. If you won't talk to me, I will camp out here."

"Then camp out there," I muttered.

"Kai, please, I need to explain. Please, baby."

"Don't call me that," I said, then realized he wasn't going anywhere and it might be easier if we just talked. "Fine. You know what? If you aren't going away, I'll give you five minutes, then you're leaving."

"Thank you," he said, coming into the small apartment.

Leslie looked between us.

"Les," I said, "could you, uh…"

She shrugged and went into what I assumed was her and May's bedroom while Silas and I stayed in the living room, both standing at some distance from each other.

"What?" I asked. "Did you forget something? Like to kick me while I was down?"

Silas' face was drawn. He looked terrible, like he'd been crying. Of course he'd been crying; it was Ellie's death anniversary. I would have loved to help him get through it, and now I felt almost guilty that this is what it all came down to.

"I'm sorry I didn't talk to you about Ellie," Silas said, taking a hesitant step forward. "I was afraid… I'm not sure of what exactly."

I stepped back. "You didn't trust me."

"No, I do trust you, angel, with my life," he insisted. "I just didn't want to burden you with this. I didn't want to make us about that. I love you so much, Kai, more than I can say, and I didn't want anything to stand between us. I didn't want to weaken those brilliant smiles of yours. I wanted to bring you happiness, not misery. I wanted to protect you, not pile this shit on you."

"Don't you see that by not telling me you've done everything you just listed?"

His face crumpled. He sat down on the sofa, looking miserable. "I'm so sorry, angel. I never meant to hurt you. I was stupid, weak, and afraid. I don't have any excuse, but I love you so much. I haven't been thinking straight, Kai."

I snorted. *Good one.*

"Can you sit, please, and look at me? I want to talk to you."

I sat down and looked at him.

"Her name was Ellie. We met in college when I was twenty-one and she was twenty-two. It was at a party. She just appeared out of nowhere and told me I had a much too serious face, then she kissed me to make it better."

"Wow," I said.

"Yeah, she was... something else. She was kind and funny and smart. She was beautiful when she smiled. She always wanted to try new things. She liked to take me on adventures. We spent... twenty years together, then some drunk asshole veered off the road and killed her on her morning run."

"Fuck," I said, taking his hand automatically.

He squeezed my hand and lifted it up to his face, kissed it, and left it there. He talked into it. "Then, for a while, I didn't even... I didn't even live. I was just doing things automatically, pushing down anything I felt for fear of feeling too much. Her parents and I got close after that and we created a tradition on the anniversary of her death. We did it for three years, and we did it for the fourth time today. We eat her favorite meal and go to the place where she was killed and leave flowers. We talk about her, sharing our memories, that kind of thing."

There were tears on his cheeks. A lump of emotion climbed up my throat, as well.

He looked at me, smiling. "Savannah asked about you, and I told her you're my partner and that I love you. I was afraid she would be angry that I replaced her daughter, but she was happy for me. She said she would like to meet you soon. James even agreed, and he rarely says anything." He chuckled at this.

I couldn't help but be intrigued. I could tell they were a big part of Silas' life, and meeting them would help me get to know him better.

Silas sighed and continued. "I know for a fact that Ellie would have loved you. She would hate seeing me mess it up and she would kick my ass right now. I've known for a while now that I'm ready to move on, Kai, that you're my love now, but I was afraid of saying the words, of saying goodbye to Ellie for good."

"You don't have to say goodbye, Silas," I whispered. "You can still love her, still remember her. I'm not replacing her. I'm only asking for you to let me in, to all of it. Ellie is a big part of who you are, so if you shut me out of that, you're not really letting me in. You don't need to love me more than her or to love *only* me, that's ridiculous. One person can love many people, and love them endlessly."

"You are too wise for your age, angel."

I rolled my eyes. "And you're too big of a doofus for your age. I would have told you all this before if you'd just talked to me. I would have supported you and come with you to the park, or I would have been fine staying home if you just explained all of this, but you just... dismissed me. You acted like you were embarrassed to be seen with me. You shut me out of your life. Even just for a day, you shut me out."

"I'm sorry," he croaked. "I'm so sorry for fucking this up. Please forgive me. Please say I can do something to fix it."

I understood Silas, I did, but I was still hurt and needed some space. "I'm staying here today and tonight. I need to think, okay? Thank you for finally telling me everything. I'll talk to you tomorrow."

Silas sniffed and looked away. He closed his eyes and nodded. "Thank you for hearing me out," he murmured. "I'll, uh, see you soon, Kai." He leaned over and kissed me on the cheek, then he left.

I was emotionally shattered.

Chapter 19

SILAS

At first, I felt like someone had sucked all the air out of my lungs. I spent a couple of hours sitting on my sofa, staring at nothing. Ellie's photo was still hidden away in a kitchen drawer from the time Kai's mother visited, so I dug it out and asked it, "What can I do, Ellie?"

She didn't answer.

"I need him back. He's all I need."

She still didn't answer.

"I messed up. Again. Remember when I used to mess up all the time? What did you tell me?" I tried to remember. "You told me that all I had to do to make you forgive me was to show you how much I cared. The devil is in the details." When I said it, the brain fog cleared out and I knew exactly what needed to be done.

***

"I'm sorry, you want me to do what now?" May asked, staring at me like I had lost my mind. I had talked to her manager and paid him handsomely. I also called a party organizer to handle all the minutia of the next day's big event, as I called it in my mind. All I needed was May's cooperation.

"I need you to get Kai here in the morning. Just come like it's any other shift and bring him with you, for muffins or whatever."

"Stew can tell him—"

"He tried, but Kai said no. He's being stubborn right now and he's probably bingeing Doctor Who episodes, and I need him here tomorrow morning."

"Goddess, why?"

"Because, I have something planned that requires his presence, and if you're as good a friend as he's told me, then you won't alert him to anything unusual happening."

She sighed, shaking her head. "More drama. Fine. I'll get him here, but you know what I'll do if you hurt him again."

"I know. Thank you."

It was not easy to arrange a proposal, especially on such short notice. If I had no money, it would have been impossible, but since I had some saved up, I decided I didn't need a big house; I just needed to propose to my boyfriend. I needed to show him that I meant business.

I called Wes last. "Hey, do you want to help me pick out a ring?"

"Wait, what?"

I loved how flabbergasted he was, and how excited as we went to pick the ring. He kept saying things like 'Kai wouldn't like that' and 'Kai would love that one.'

"How do you know Kai that well?" I asked.

He shrugged. "You really get to know someone when you're doing repetitive work and chatting about everything under the sun. I also know his sign, his favorite ice cream, his spirit animal, what you did for Valentine's Day, and so on. Not to mention the art. I know his style better than he does. Really, I know him better than you do, so you better listen to me."

I did. I got the ring Wes suggested.

All I had to do was actually pull it off the next day and pray to every god that would listen that my love says yes and I get to keep him.

***

KAI

May was acting weirder than usual, but I chalked it up to not having sex with her girlfriend on account of me being in their apartment. I'd slept on the sofa and had a kink in my neck and bad coffee in my hand. Leslie made it, and I was convinced the only reason May didn't tell her it was bad was because she loved her. How much would you have to love someone to drink coffee that bad every day, though?

May made me go to work with her so I wouldn't mope around all day. She said she'd make me her new favorite coffee smoothie, which sounded intriguing, provided it was not accompanied by any spells.

"No spells," I reminded her when we got there.

"No spells, I promise," she said.

She unlocked the door, and we were greeted by a Doctor Who convention.

What the...?

There was a TARDIS in the corner. An actual, life-sized, real TARDIS. A bunch of mugs lined up on the counter and in people's hands were TARDIS-shaped. Everything was blue and flashy, blinding me, except for the one person in the whole place

187

who was dressed like the Doctor. Silas had a striped suit on and gel in his hair, making it stick out.

It was so hot.

I blinked, trying to dispel the strange mirage, but it persisted. I noticed Wes and Jazz sitting at a table to the right, having coffee. Jason and Matthew were at another table. I turned to May, who was smirking.

"Traitor," I hissed.

She shrugged and went to join Jason and Matthew while I walked up to Silas in a daze. "Have you lost your mind?" I asked him.

Smiling, he took my hands and said, "On the contrary. The day I met you, Kai, I regained my senses. My heart started to beat again. You breathed life into my lungs and purpose into my heart. Like I've said before, you're my angel. You healed me with your smiles. Your goofy smiles, your bashful smiles, your nervous smiles, your happy smiles, your sad smiles. Every smile you possess, I have loved. I hope you'll forgive my blunder, as sometimes I make mistakes, but I try to fix them as best and fast as I can. Because you're the best thing that's ever happened to me, baby." He paused, giving me a loving and nervous look, making me wonder what he was up to. "At this point, I just have one question."

He dropped to one knee.

I gasped.

He opened a velvet box with two stunning bands. "Does it need saying?"

I burst into tearful laughter. He just quoted one of my favorite scenes in Doctor Who, where the Doctor almost professes his love for Rose Tyler.

"Oh, my god. I mean... wow."

"Is that a yes, baby?"

Fuck this. I tugged at his collar, dragging him to his feet, and jumped at him, so he could pick me up like he liked to. I hoped

I didn't break the rings or something, but I didn't care at that moment. "Yes, yes, yes," I said, laughing and crying at the same time, clutching at him with both my arms and legs.

Then, I unclutched myself and beamed at him.

He took my face and kissed me.

Everyone clapped and cheered. I'd forgotten that we had an audience! Despite this, Silas kissed me deeply, holding my head so tight I thought he was afraid I would change my mind or something and try to run away. I reassured him with my kiss and my eyes and with my arms wrapped around him. Soon, he seemed to relax.

My baby. My daddy.

Now, my fiancé.

As we celebrated our engagement, I didn't forget to whisper in his ear, "You're evil, you know, getting dressed like that. I want to fuck you so bad."

His eyes went wide. "Could you have waited to tell me this later, maybe?"

"Then I'd be the only one suffering."

"So, that's what I'm in for," he said, smirking.

"Shared misery. It's called marriage. Look it up, babe."

"Uh huh," he said, then kissed my temple.

That day, I felt loved, cherished, and appreciated. Silas showed me the best way he knew how that he loved me. Maybe we weren't perfect, but we loved each other fiercely, and that was a pretty good foundation for spending our lives together.

"Does it need saying?" I asked.

"It doesn't," he answered.

From that day on, that was our new way of saying I love you.

Wait!

Thank you for reading Kai's Healing Smiles.

It would mean the world if you could take 2 minutes to leave a review on Amazon and Goodreads.

Also, please turn the page to find a sneak peek of my next novel **To Trust and To Touch**.

I appreciate you!

Sneak Peek

ALEX

It's Wednesday, my night at Kink World, and I'm running late. I have to speed my bike through a couple of intersections, but I come out unscathed. I could die about a dozen ways riding like this. I know it won't be that easy, though. When I go, it won't be soon and it won't be easy. It's someone else, who is lucky. I've never been lucky in my fucking life.

I almost crash into the building's entrance, regain my balance, and tie the bike to a nearby rack. Quick as lightning, I sprint to the entrance and knock three times. A small window opens. "Pass?"

I roll my eyes. "It's me, Frank, open up."

The window closes and the big gate opens, revealing a smirking individual. "Oh, you're still with us, are you, Shade?"

Shade is my pseudonym at Kink World. My stage name, if you will.

"As long as there are greedy, horny fuckers in the world, I'll always be employed, my friend."

Frank scoffs and lets me pass. I practically run through the few people that have already populated the club at this early hour—*losers*—and head for the secret entrance to the second level. I run my ID card and the light turns green. Then, I take the stairs two at a time under the dim red light, sweating like a pig, but whatever. It might actually come out in my favor when I start working myself up.

The second level of Kink World is for the fuckers who like to watch. The peepers, the perverts, or whatever you want to call them. They usually have specific kinks, and they pay extra to have them available. I'm not doing this for them, though. I'm doing it for the money. It's the only gig that pays as well, and I still can't believe the owner lets me do it solo.

If I had to do it with a partner, I'd be out of here in two seconds flat.

The second-floor changing room is empty other than me because I'm late; the watchers are probably waiting, frustrated. I quickly change into my skimpy outfit and jump into my designated room—number fifteen. It is bare except for a big master bed in the middle and a table with all kinds of props. There's lube, dildos of every size and type, butt plugs, et cetera. I'm required to use at least three items per scene, per my agreement.

Oh, yeah, I signed a contract and everything, but I insisted on a clause that no one is allowed to touch me. No one who works here and none of the patrons. If someone does, I can call security.

I was impressed with Mason's professionalism, to be honest, though I guess you don't get to own a club like this without being a professional. I just regret there aren't more slots in the week. If I could, I would just work here and quit my stupid Starbucks job. Oh well.

Getting paid to play with yourself for an hour is a good gig.

I look at the big one-way mirror on the wall, on the other side of which the onlookers are. I wink and tease them because I can. They're never going to get anything else from me, so I might as well make this good for them.

I take my place on the bed and sprawl my legs so that everything is visible. I let out a deep sigh and prepare to give the fuckers the show of a lifetime. I'm already strung up because I haven't jerked off in more than a day, and the resulting orgasm is going to be mental.

Good. It might mean more tips, too.

Slowly, sensually, I start the program. It's an hour of my time, pleasuring myself, letting strangers watch.

Those fuckers.

They can watch, but they will never touch.

***

Just as I head to the bar for the one free drink that's included in my contract, I feel a hand on my shoulder. I turn around—fuck, of course it's Daniel. He's a rich businessman who always wears fancy suits and sits up in the VIP section, which is why I don't go there anymore. Did he sneak up on me on purpose?

"Hello, pretty thing. How about I buy you a drink?"

"I've told you, man, you're wasting your time," I say as I slip away from his grasp and continue on my way.

Unfortunately, he follows me to the bar. "Why are you being so difficult, baby? I just want to talk to you."

"No thanks."

"Come on, there must be something you want."

"I want you to fucking leave me alone," I bark and wave the bartender, Nate, who already knows what my order is. He nods, smiling.

Shit, I can't even fucking relax because the fucker is still near; I can feel him.

"Let me make you feel good, baby," he hisses in my ear.

I jerk around and say, "I'm not your fucking baby. Go away."

He laughs, the fucker. "This is fun for you, isn't it? Teasing the men with your tight little ass and making them work hard for it. Well, darling, you won't meet anyone who's going to work harder than me." He leans closer, invading my personal space, licking his lips, and his gross fingers envelop my wrist.

Oh, hell no!

In a matter of seconds, I pull out of his grip and twist his arm behind his back, pushing him to his knees. He yells bloody murder.

People around us look and someone mighty big pulls me aside and barks, "Shade, what the fuck, man?" It's one of the security guys. "Get out of here and get some fucking air."

Of course. Because this fucker paid to be here and I didn't, so I'm disposable, but their precious members aren't.

"Whatever," I mutter, then leave through the front entrance because it's closer. I don't want to think about the stupid prick or his sleazy hands on my body. Fuck! They always find a way to touch me.

Trying not to shake too badly, I get out a cigarette and light it. There's a huge line on one side of the entrance, so I stand on the other side, leaning against the wall, trying to calm down as I struggle with my shitty lighter. Fuck, come on, damn it, light up.

As the smoke billows, calm engulfs me and I can finally breathe again.

There's another guy there, busy talking on his phone, so I focus on the stupid breathing exercises my therapist gave me. I would much rather punch someone, but I wouldn't be paid in that case, so I just count backwards from one hundred. It's not like he could have hurt me, I know that. I've trained in five different types of martial arts, so you're not likely to get the drop on me in this lifetime, no matter how big you are. I could even take on two or three guys, as long as they're not military-trained or something like that. The problem isn't the inappropriate touching or the threat of more. The problem is the flashes, the memories, the fucking things that always keep me from hooking up with anybody.

It's been three years since a man touched me.

I mean, in a sexual way.

To get release, I have to use toys and my hand. Sometimes, I close my eyes and pretend I have someone with me, but it rarely works, which means most of the time, I am really fucking strung up. Like right now.

"Daddy loves you too, sweetheart," the man on the phone says. He's tall with wide shoulders, short, dark hair, a soft smile, tidy clothes, and scruff on his chin. Probably in his forties because of those lines around his eyes, but the smile makes him look younger and more attractive than he actually is. He doesn't look like a rich asshole. More like a regular guy, which is another point in his favor.

Suddenly, I realize what I'm doing. What the fuck? I don't know him, and I don't want to know him.

"Yes, baby, Daddy can't wait to come back home and read you a story." He pauses, then the lines around his eyes pinch as he smiles. "Yes, your favorite one, princess."

So, he's straight. All right, then. A strange feeling fills my chest, then I realize that feeling disappointed over a stranger's sexual orientation is ridiculous.

I'll pretend it was heartburn.

"Tell Uncle Dave to make dinner. No pizza, all right?"

Uh, is this a menage kind of thing? And who the fuck calls their partner *uncle*?

"Kisses, baby. I'll see you tonight. Get Uncle Dave on the phone." He pauses again, then his tone changes, and the sweetness drains away with the flick of a switch. "If you order pizza again, I will smother you in your sleep, got it? She needs to eat nutritional food, not the shit you give her." Another few moments of silence while he rubs his hand across his forehead and pinches the bridge of his nose. "Fine, I'm sorry. Thank you for taking care of her while I'm out *wilding*, to use your words, but I really just want you to make sure—" He stops abruptly, then lets out an exasperated huff and rolls his eyes. "Jesus, all right. I don't care about the twinks inside. I just want to know my daughter is well taken care of."

I snort.

He looks at me, surprised to see someone watching him. "Dave, I have to go. I'll see you later, all right?" He uses all of a short pause to glare at me. "Yeah, bye."

He hangs up, frowning.

I give him one of my famous smirks, challenging him to say something.

"Do you always eavesdrop on people's conversations?"

"Only if they say words like daddy and twink."

His eyes grow wide as he realizes where the fuck he is standing, then groans. "Jesus, did you think I was talking to—"

"Your sexy baby girl? Yep."

He looks like he's going to gag. "Great, now I feel sick, and I'll probably never come back here again, if this is what I get."

I laugh. "I mean, what did you expect? We're in front of a sex club."

"In my defense, I was just about to step into said club when my phone rang, and I didn't think having this conversation inside would go very well." The guy shakes his head, a smile playing at his lips. At least he has a sense of humor.

I puff out a ring of smoke, then another.

He looks me over. "Why aren't you inside?"

I shrug. "I'm done with it for tonight. You?"

"Oh, I have to go in or my brother will possibly disown me."

"Who's your brother?" I ask, cursing my curiosity. Why do I even want to know shit like that? He's just another fucker I don't want to know, who I don't want to touch me, and who I'll never see again. Period.

"Mason," he says.

Damn. "The owner?"

"Yes, and let's just say that not coming here for five years means to him that I am a sexually repressed bastard who needs to get laid." He shakes his head. "I don't know why I said that to a complete stranger."

I shrug. "No worries, I can keep a secret."

"Great, thanks," he says, but his smile resurfaces. "You're one of those people who are easy to talk to, aren't you? You probably collect people's secrets as currency so you can blackmail them later."

My eyebrows go way up. "Are you a millionaire or something? Because otherwise, I wouldn't bother blackmailing your old ass."

"I'm forty, not seventy."

"Happy fucking birthday, then."

He laughs, shaking his head again. It's fun to talk to him.

"So, why are you repressed, anyway? Haven't you got a twink or two on speed dial? All the smart daddies are doing it."

"Ah, no. I had Emma—my daughter—five years ago. Let's just say I've only been spending time with her and various cartoon characters."

"No shit? So, you've been hibernating."

"Something like that," he says, rubbing the back of his neck. He looks even more attractive when he's embarrassed, but I shouldn't care about that.

"I can't imagine." I puff more rings of smoke.

"No, I don't imagine you can."

There's something in his tone I don't like.

"You shouldn't make snap judgments based on people's appearances, you know," I say, thinking of what he sees before him—a skinny, wiry guy with vine tattoos all over his arms, legs, and torso, not that he can see it all. I am covered in barbed wire, basically. You can't touch or you'll get stung.

"I suppose that's fair," he says. "And what about you? Did you get everything you wanted out of Kink World tonight?"

I let out a breath, thinking about my miserable night. Playing with myself in front of strangers and then getting accosted by some asshole. A night like any other.

"I got what I came for," I say.

Pursing his lips, he nods.

While he's silent, I examine him more closely; not that I should. His clothes are not ideal for clubbing. He's wearing a long-sleeved button down and khaki slacks held up with a leather belt. An expensive-looking watch flashes from his wrist, which will probably get stolen inside. His face looks warm and soft, his brown eyes adding to the effect.

Everything about him screams *safe*.

If I wanted someone, I would ask him out. I would keep flirting with him and tease him until he got the message and we went somewhere for drinks. But not the club. Fuck the club.

Unfortunately, I am who I am, and I don't date or fuck anymore.

"So, I should go inside and face the music," he says.

Oh, good. That saves me from having to rudely walk away, as I always do.

"Good luck with your wilding, man," I say, giving him one last teasing smirk, which I am famous for. "Make sure to get it all out."

He snorts. "I'll try, but no promises."

I wink at him and watch him walk away, then he turns and gives me another curious look before the club swallows him whole.

Well, that was weird.

***

Author's Note: **To Trust and To Touch** *is a standalone m/m romance that will be published on December 13, 2022. You can pre-order it now or subscribe to the author's newsletter for updates.*

Acknowledgments

Special thanks go to my editor, B. K. Bass, who made this book readable. I tend to ramble and make stupid mistakes, and a good editor makes the whole thing flow while keeping the tone, which is what B. K. did, and beautifully.

Also, thank you to Ruart, who made the stunning illustration of Silas and Kai in the beginning of the book. It's the perfect depiction of those two, and she just knew intuitively how they look together.

Finally, a very special thanks to YOU, my precious reader, who is brave enough to venture into a story written by a first-time author. I appreciate you more than I can ever say. You're the reason I write.

www.ingramcontent.com/pod-product-compliance
Lightning Source LLC
LaVergne TN
LVHW041513170726
843492LV00005B/1485